AGENT RED-FATAL JUSTICE

TEAGAN STONE BOOK 4

AVA S. KING

304 PUBLISHING COMPANY

INTRODUCTION

Sign-up to Ava S. King's mailing list for news, new releases and special offers.

https://landing.mailerlite.com/webforms/landing/r7j2s6

*I want to dedicate this book to my family and friends.
You are always with me, no matter where I go, and
everything you've taught me has made me a better person.*

DISCLAIMER

This work of fiction contains strong language and explicit content and is only intended for mature readers. This story may contain unconventional situations, language, and sexual encounters that may offend some readers. This book is for mature readers (18+).

SYNOPSIS

Teagan Stone is out of options and quickly running out of time. She must find the creator of America's most sought-after device to save America from a potential attack. But devious Russian forces with deep pockets are impenetrable.

The seasoned spy will stop at nothing to find the creator, bring his kidnappers to justice, and prevent a bombing—even if it means she has to risk her life.

She refuses to let evildoers take innocent lives. Not on her watch.

ONE

The alarm blared, and the team secured their masks and guns within five minutes to save the hostages from a terrorist attack. Teagan stood behind the two-way mirror and watched the clock run down with top members of the president's cabinet as Spider, Daughtrey, Gregory, and a few other seasoned team members rushed through. After climbing in from each side of the plane simulation, her breathing stayed elevated. Seeing Gregory lift the bottom shaft of the plane near the rear door, dressed in all black, he signaled to Spider that he would take the right side of the aisle. Spider strolled down the walkway with his gun ready to claim a terrorist. Soon as he hit the second row of seats, a man jumped up in camouflage, reaching for a hostage. When Spider raised his gun and shot at his chest, the red dye exploded.

"One down, two to go," Spider whispered through his headpiece.

"I got first-class secure," Daughtrey muttered back, opening the door of the bathroom.

Teagan gleaned at the clock, and it read two minutes left.

"Keep it moving," Teagan mumbled to herself.

All eyes were on them, and if they wanted to continue The Firm, they needed to show it was worth paying over five hundred million dollars a year to keep them running.

"It's a waste of money," Duncan Brooks, Deputy Secretary of Defense, said. The blond blue-eyed, skinny, cocky, five-eleven, preppy boy was a pain in everyone's ass. He crossed his arms and shook his head. For his entire career in politics, Duncan had taken every chance he'd gotten to shut down the agency. A few of the guys chuckled at his comment when he announced another call that a second guy was taken down. With forty seconds left, every breath was held in the room as Duncan and Teagan exchanged a look. Accomplishing this task of securing more funding, eventually picking someone to take over as director would help Teagan get closer to finally head into retirement officially. She was still grappling with some of her memories. Life had gotten only more complicated after the death of Abe Price. Sandra Gregg made it her mission to make Teagan aware that she was on to what The Firm did with killing, kidnapping, and brutalizing enemies of the United States.

"Time," Teagan called out, releasing her hand from the buzzer. Clapping in accomplishing her goal, Teagan smirked, seeing Duncan roll his eyes and gaining the needed funding for another five years.

Duncan cleared his throat and extended his hand for a shake.

"Good job, Stone."

Teagan looked down at his hand and backed up to Duncan.

"Thanks." She reached out and clasped his hand, then turned toward the door and headed to the room with her crew.

Spider removed the headset, wiping the sweat off his brow.

"What did they say?" Spider removed his gloves.

"Nothing yet." Teagan motioned at the two-way mirror.

"Funny how the guys in suits determine if we get to do our jobs, one they're too scared to do," Gregory complained, shaking his head.

Teagan thought the same thing as the email came in yesterday morning while working on a fresh case. Before she could call the president to discuss the budget renewal, grumblings throughout Congress put them in Duncan's crosshairs.

"I'm starving; how long do we have to wait?" Daughtrey pointed at the window as the door opened, and Duncan, followed by the other top aides, came back into the room.

"Gentleman and lady, you've shown your skills, and the president, as you know, is fond of whatever it is you do here." Duncan waved his hand around.

"You mean saving lives?" Gregory's brow lifted in confusion.

Spider and Daughtrey chuckled as Duncan cleared his throat.

"If that's what you want to call it. If it were up to me, I would shut this entire organization down." Duncan shrugged, sliding his hands in his pocket. All eyes looked around the room, then back at him in surprise.

"Are we free to go or not?" Daughtrey crossed his arms over his chest. Teagan put her hand on his chest, stepping in front of him and facing Duncan.

"What's your problem?" Teagan asked.

"My problem is people like you come in and use up resources that could be used for actual work to get done," Duncan argued, pointing his finger in her face. Teagan held a harsh glare, picking up on every little detail of Duncan's face and demeanor. Something about the crust wedged in the corner of his eyes let her know he wasn't getting enough sleep. The wrinkled grey coat that was two sizes too big hung from his tall, thin, lanky frame. The yellow color of his teeth, unshaven beard, and dirty nails screamed the lack of detail to his hygiene and appearance of a man either going through a divorce or about to lose his job.

"When did she serve you papers?" Teagan questioned.

He looked her up and down, nose flared.

"What did you say?"

"I asked when did your wife serve you papers for a divorce?" Teagan repeated, not backing down. The guys sneaked behind her.

"My private life has nothing to do with this shitstorm of a team. Do you know how many times we've gotten calls about a corporation or unlawful detainment?" Duncan blurted out.

"Either we get the budget, or we don't. You have too much on your plate at the moment. The president will reach out when he needs us," Teagan replied, walking off and nodding for the guys to follow as she went around Duncan toward the front entrance and pushed it open.

"Agent Stone?" Duncan called out. Teagan stood face forward with her back to him. "Don't get too comfortable." Duncan left through the other side of the office. Teagan headed to the truck, opening the door as Spider came up beside her.

"You playing dirty now, Teagan?" Spider removed his vest and helmet and passed them to the cleanup detail of the facility, loading up the truck as the driver started the car. Gregory and Daughtrey followed.

"Spider, you know me better than anyone. Duncan is the one playing dirty."

"That doesn't mean we stoop to his level." Spider sighed, buckling his seatbelt.

"Are we going to eat? I'm still hungry from breakfast." Daughtrey stood at the second SUV, waiting to get in the driver's side. He hated being driven around like the rest of the team, even though Teagan constantly fussed about them getting more and more notices.

"Keeping my eyes open. Let's go so we can feed this big baby," Teagan kidded, smiling at Daughtrey. Until she learned something different, Duncan would be on her list of people who might become a problem.

"Did you get any more intelligence on Maksim?" Spider inquired, loosening the seatbelt over his chest and checking his messages. Teagan looked back at him through the rearview mirror, raising a brow.

"No, have any of your contacts turned up?" Teagan thought, tapping her fingers on her thigh. The last known contact after Maksim getting away after the shootout was months ago, and Russian intel dried up, so Teagan focused on other open cases of potential threats to the country.

"Soon as I get back to the office, I'll put in some calls." Spider stretched out with his arm on the back of the seat.

SEEING the stack of papers on the Petrov crime family, Teagan flipped through files and reports the FBI tried to keep hidden. Most of the details were blacked out in Sharpie or classified but pinpointing the death counts amassed with his family getting away made her heart pump faster.

"Bastard."

Maksim was last known in Russia, and not having any guidance from their government on turning him over would make the task of getting him stateside even worse. Grabbing her cup of iced latte from Starlights Cafe from the local café, Teagan sipped on her drink, staring at photos of Maksim talking with another man in front of a car.

"Where are you?"

Gritting her teeth, Teagan sat back in her seat, studying the photos for any hint that would give her something to go on. Her first case a year ago was Diablo, moving right into stopping an assassination attempt, to being accused of killing a reporter, and now handling a corrupt gun ring in New York. Taking her skills to the streets and talking with local gangs and police officers might benefit from getting Maksim in custody faster. His facial expression looked stark, determined, and ready for war. Knocking at her door, she turned in her seat. The door opened with Broderick progressing inside.

"Yeah."

"I think we've walked on eggshells, and I wanted to come to some agreement."

She motioned for him to take a seat in front of her desk.

"Speak." Teagan put the photos down on her desk.

"You probably have an idea about me being some corrupt asshole."

"Pretty much."

"Noted, but you have to understand after you left, they put me in charge."

"Are you telling me you didn't enjoy having the responsibility to call the shots?"

"I regret some choices and believe Stanton was one of them."

"He played everyone. Then sleeping with Leah caused me to look the other way." Broderick clasped his hands together in his lap. Broderick was clever and careful with his words. Teagan would keep watch on how Broderick moved forward but let him take on more responsibility unless he made another move on her family.

"We'll never be friends, Broderick. You broke that trust." Her phone ringing interrupted the conversation.

"Director Stone."

"Am I speaking with someone from The Firm?" a whisper-soft voice said over the phone.

Teagan's brow rose in confusion.

"You're on with Director Stone. How can I help you?"

Broderick stood to leave, but she waved him to stay and put the call on speakerphone.

"I can't talk long, or they'll know it's me," she responded.

"Who is this?" Teagan picked up her pen and paper to take notes.

"I know who's helping Maksim Petrov."

Broderick and Teagan's eyes locked in sync at the statement.

"What's your name?" Teagan questioned.

"Sorry, I can't tell you that," the voice whispered slowly.

"What can you tell me?"

"All I can say is he can't be trusted. My brother got into something stupid, and now I'm worried about him," the girl said.

"Who is your brother?" Teagan rose out of her seat, hovering over the phone.

"He doesn't understand that the money comes with loyalty to the Petrov family."

"Tell me your name," Teagan replied. Broderick crossed his arms over his chest. Her door opened again, and Spider walked in with Tony behind him.

"I need to go," she said, rushing off the phone. Teagan's eyes closed shut, her head lowered in frustration.

"Interrupting something?" Spider asked.

"You want me to trace the call?" Broderick inquired.

"Please and make sure you keep it under wraps until we know for sure who's behind this call. It could be a setup."

Broderick picked up her phone and called Gregory. For a second, Teagan estimated the person had to have known her schedule. Often, her lunch break would be right around this time. Broderick ended the call, holding a piece of paper.

"It's untraceable," Broderick said, and Teagan cursed under her breath.

Spider started to speak, and Teagan raised her hand, cutting him off.

"I just got a call from some woman who said she knows about the Maksim Petrov family."

"She didn't give a name." Spider's face wore a scowl.

Broderick shook his head.

"By the time Teagan tried to get them to give a name, they hung up, and we didn't have time to set up any tracing capabilities," Broderick said.

Teagan moved toward the stack of files and passed over half of what she was working on toward Spider. Until they called again, it'd be back to the simple task of reading and studying what they knew so far of Petrov and reports from her contacts in the city.

"Broderick set up a meeting with Malcolm Holmes of

the Third Street gang," Teagan explained, writing something on a piece of paper.

"Are we ordering lunch in?" Spider questioned.

Teagan glanced at the clock on the wall. She had promised a family dinner tonight. Burying herself deep in work lately, she would make it up to them with pizza and a movie.

"I can't today. I promised the kids pizza and a movie." Teagan lifted her jacket off the coatrack and picked up her purse and some files to leave for the rest of the day.

"Should we expect you tomorrow?" Spider asked.

"You can handle one day in charge. Call me if you need me." Teagan patted him on the chest and strolled out of her office.

"Tony, let's go," Teagan called over her shoulder.

<h1 style="text-align:center">TWO</h1>

An hour later, Teagan slid her key in the door of the quiet house and tossed her purse on the couch, releasing a breath over the long day. Heading to the kitchen to grab a bottle of water, she heard laughter coming from the backyard. The kids were playing with Christian on the swing set. Grabbing the cordless phone off the charger, she went out to the backyard and chuckled at Tatum, screaming at how high she was on the swing.

"Mommy." Cole ran toward Teagan and hugged her legs.

She lifted him up in her arms and kissed his cheek.

"How's my baby doing?"

"Good," Cole replied and kissed her cheek, and she put him down on his feet.

"You're home early," Christian observed.

"Yep, pizza and movie tonight." Teagan raised the cordless phone in the air. All the kids screamed in excitement.

"Who wants pepperoni and cheese pizza?" Teagan asked, dialing the local pizza shop.

"Me! Me!" Cole and Tatum jumped up and down.

Teagan leaned over to cup Tatum's chin and inhaled her baby girl's sweet vanilla scent from her hair shampoo. Christian stretched his arm around her neck when she stood and pulled her into his arms, kissing her behind her ear.

"How was your day?" Teagan tucked a piece of her hair behind her ear and followed the kids into the house. Christian shut and locked the back door, turning to Teagan.

"Mostly researching potential clients I could bring with me if I start my own company."

He released her from his hold and opened the fridge to grab a bottle of water.

"Do you want anything specific on your pizza?"

"Meat lovers and hot wings." Christian leaned against the counter. Tatum ran back into the kitchen, reaching her arms out for him to pick her up.

"Make it two large pizzas and hot wings."

"Mommy, can you do my hair tonight?" Tatum asked.

"Yes, baby. Just let Mommy finish her work first."

Heading back into the living room, CJ and Cole were searching through the stack of movies. Teagan was proud to see her family content and happy that she was home with them.

"The pizza will be here soon." Teagan sat on the couch with CJ laying in her lap, stroking his head.

"Mommy, are you a cop?" CJ questioned, eyeing her.

"No, why would you ask that?"

Cole turned on *Spiderman* and sat in front of the coffee table next to Tatum. The doorbell rang, and he popped up, running to beat Christian to the door.

"Pizza!"

"You know better than to answer the door," Christian

said, pulling his wallet out of his pocket. Taking the pizza from the driver, he let Cole handle the bag of hot wings.

"Set it on the table, and I'll grab some plates." Christian placed the pizza boxes down on the coffee table, ignoring the conversation between Teagan and CJ.

"Some of the kids at my school talked about seeing you in the news," CJ explained, rising from her lap and scooting close to the pizza.

"Ignore those kids. I have a job that's important and protects you."

"So, something like a cop?"

"Eat your pizza."

"Who's ready to eat?" Christian came back in with a gallon of lemonade.

"Don't get any grease on the table, you guys." Teagan helped to plate their food with equal slices of pizza and wings. The kids giggled as Teagan sat back on the couch, eating a piece of pizza. She cuddled up next to Christian again just as the house phone rang.

"I'll get it," Christian said, reaching around her and grabbing the phone off the end table.

"She's right here. Hold on," Christian's low voice hissed in annoyance as he passed her the phone.

"Who is it?"

"Work."

Teagan caught the hint of annoyance in Christian's response and rose off the couch, heading toward her office.

"HELLO."

"Sorry to bug you, Teagan, but I thought you'd want to

know what's happening," Gregory said. Teagan locked her office door once inside, taking a seat behind her desk. Turning her computer on, she logged into the database of The Firm.

"What do you have?"

"The call wasn't traceable, but we have other information from Malcolm," Gregory answered.

"How did that conversation go?"

"He wasn't on board at first, but after a little persuasion and threatening to lock his people up, he agreed," Gregory hinted.

"So, is he dealing with Maksim?"

"He told him he wasn't, but I don't fully trust him."

Teagan opened her desk drawer, removing the black binder with every contact with criminals she'd come across in her line of work. She wanted to check her files on Malcolm from the last time they'd spoken.

"Malcolm's still running illegal gambling rings." Teagan clicked on the photos of Malcolm talking with other men surrounded by women in skimpy lingerie. The images brought back memories of her time with Diablo in Spain. The amount of attention he poured on her that night made her heart swell in the thought that he was really in love with her and wanted a future, but she knew it was all make believe for a mission.

Gregory brought her out of her daze. "What are you thinking?"

"Make the call and get him to meet with me."

"In public?"

"At the park."

"Should I have Spider with you or—"

"Call Broderick."

"All right."

They hung up, and Teagan went through her updated emails from Spider about the budget numbers. She desperately wanted to hire more security and get training to add to the team for missions. In her vision, it would be best to have the top people recruited so she could officially step back and put someone else in charge. A knock at her door came, and she jumped up to open the door. Pushing the door wider, he stepped inside, passing her favorite lemon and honey tea toward her.

"What's this?"

Christian leaned against the corner of the desk, watching Teagan drink her tea and closing the space between them. Staring into her eyes, Christian lifted her chin and ran a hand down her arm.

"I knew you'd be up all night working. We haven't had a second to connect."

"How is everything going?"

"Busy."

"I know you're building your business. Do you think it's too much?"

"Not really; I have a few partners that I'm bringing on to invest."

"Does this mean we're going to have less time together? The kids are getting bigger."

"Maybe a family vacation should happen."

"CJ wants to go to the opening baseball game. Maybe we could do that first."

"He'd love that, and Tatum wants to go to Disney World."

Teagan placed the tea on the desk, reached up to hold the back of Christian's neck, and pressed a kiss on his lips.

"Let's go to bed."

"Reconnect." Christian tapped her on the nose.

"Mmmm... Big time."

TWO DAYS LATER, Teagan stepped out of the dark-tinted van holding a cup of tea in her hand, wearing her black shades. She approached Malcolm sitting on top of the park bench, smoking a cigar with his security surrounding him. Malcolm Holmes was thirty-eight years old, five-ten, dark-brown skin, bushy brow, thin nose, and muscular build. He was known in the city as the Godfather for helping local kids get into school and donating money to local businesses to keep them afloat. People didn't know he was the biggest ringleader over guns and gambling in the city. Crime was at an all-time high in New York, specifically Queens, and many times they'd arrested or buried people who had some affiliation with him.

"Mr. Holmes." Teagan lifted her shades to the top of her head.

He grinned, stepping off the bench and puffing on the cigar as he extended his hand.

"Teagan Stone."

"You know why I'm here."

"Gregory told me."

"So, are you going to help?"

They walked down the walkway toward the pond as the security followed them. The weather was cool and breezy with the sun streaming down. A few people were out playing, and mother groups exercised with their babies.

"You know Maksim and what he's capable of doing." Malcolm stopped moving and turned to face her with his hands in his pockets.

"We can protect you." Teagan sipped on her tea.

"How long have you been married?" Malcolm questioned.

"Stick to why we're here."

"The loyalty you have with your husband is the same thing I have with my team."

"Do you know why you're able to run around right now?" He scoffed and ran a hand down his face.

"Does that make you feel good to threaten me?" Malcolm stepped in closer to her face.

"If you're scared, say that." Malcolm laughed, clapping his hands.

"Agent Stone, we're done here."

"We're done when I say we're done. You will help us, Mr. Holmes."

"If I don't?"

The unfortunate thing about her job was to threaten people she felt weren't necessarily guilty, but she needed to show that she was in charge to get her point across.

"Teagan, everything all right?" She noticed the grimace across Malcolm's face when Broderick came up beside her.

"He's your backup?" Malcolm pointed at Broderick.

"Broderick is going to be your contact from now on. If Maksim so much as breathes, I want to know about it."

"What am I getting out of this?"

"Staying out of jail," Broderick said.

Malcolm's security tried to lunge at Broderick, but Malcolm held a hand up to stop them.

"Let me get this straight. You want me to help you capture a Russian terrorist and not care about my safety."

Even though he seemed confident in his words, she could tell Malcolm was scared shitless. Maksim was a more significant threat to him. He could wipe out his entire bloodline with one phone call.

"All we need is for you to tell us when he makes contact with you," Broderick replied.

Malcolm glanced over at the group of moms holding their kids and dumped his cigar on the ground, stomping the fire out.

"I'm not wearing a wire," Malcolm said.

"I want Broderick to be there with you, and he'll wear the wire. Assume he's one of your security guys," Teagan explained.

"He's going to know something's up if he was on my security detail. He looks like the police," Malcolm complained, throwing his hands up.

"Don't worry about what I'm wearing. Just let everyone know I'm your new guard," Broderick stated. The male ego between the two of them had Teagan shaking her head in disbelief. No matter what, men always wanted to be the top dog in any fight.

"Broderick will be fine. Keep us updated." Teagan extended her hand out for a handshake.

He nodded, reaching out his palm to seal the deal, and grunted at Broderick as he walked off. She peered at Malcolm and his team as the car drove away, finishing off her drink.

"Are you up for this?" Teagan studied Broderick. The small scar over his brow still stood out even after five years. Why couldn't she forgive and forget? They'd been at odds since she joined the team and believed all those years it was a true friendship, but the kidnapping of her family changed everything.

"Don't tell me you're scared for me." Broderick glanced over, joking. Teagan smirked and strolled to her awaiting security detail. She lifted one leg into the car, turned to her right side, and watched Broderick grinning as he walked backward toward his red Range Rover. They'd been enemies for the longest time. His irresistible grin kept women falling at his feet. Not Teagan Stone. Behind the mask was a man who only wanted things his way, and in time, this case would show what his next moves were.

THREE

A week later.

Malcolm sat in a room with his team surrounding him as Broderick stood to the side with a wire on him, capturing everything they talked about. One of the conditions he made after leaving the meeting with Teagan was that any discussions beyond Maksim weren't used against him and his men. At first, Teagan wouldn't agree, but Malcolm was adamant about not letting Broderick in on anything if his people got arrested. They even agreed to allow deals to go down and not interfere unless Maksim was a part of everything.

"Who's this guy?" Ishmael, one of his lower-level dealers, motioned at Broderick.

Malcolm looked over his shoulder.

"This is Brody, one of my new security men."

"Is something going on?" Ishmael's brow dipped in concern.

"Nothing beside us moving in higher rank with some new clients." Malcolm moseyed around the table of men. They were all inside the backroom of Sammy's restaurant, a local cafe that Malcolm invested in when they went under. With the investment, he was allowed to use their back room anytime he wanted without argument. Now five of his top lieutenants sat waiting to get word on any updates. He cut his eyes toward Broderick, standing like a statue, not saying anything.

"How is the money looking on third and bankman?"

"I picked up a hundred thousand from Beans earlier today," Ishmael replied, lifting the bag off the floor and throwing it on the table.

"What about you, Ralph?" Malcolm said, checking the bag of money.

Ralph was older. He recently got out of prison for drug trafficking after five years and came out wanting to make money again to take care of his family.

"We brought up two hundred thousand. I need more of the Glocks," Ralph responded, passing over two duffel bags.

"Have Dorian load you up with some new pieces. I called you all here for a reason."

"What's up?" Ishmael called out.

"I got a phone call from Maksim Petrov." Malcolm tapped his finger on the table, peering a look at Broderick.

"Isn't he the Russian dude?" Ishmael said.

"He's interested in doing business together."

"How much is he paying?"

"He wants a cut on gambling and gun traffic." Everyone in the room grumbled, talking all over each other.

"We run the gambling, and we're not working for some Russian family," Ishmael barked, jumping up out of his seat.

"For real, boss. We have the entire west and east on lock," Declan said. He was one of his lower soldiers who stayed on top of his gambling business.

"Exactly, why bring more noise on us and put the DEA

on our asses for fucking with Russians?" Ishmael argued, pacing back and forth.

"Do you trust me?" Malcolm questioned the entire room, staring at each man he brought on throughout the years. The community of kids looked up to him, but the older men and women knew Malcolm wasn't any good, and he only continued to hurt the community with the influx of drugs, gambling, and guns.

Ralph cleared his throat.

"Who do we report to if he comes onboard?"

"Nothing changes. I'm still holding all the cards," Malcolm explained.

Ishmael nodded, leaning against the wall with his arms folded across his chest.

"Then let's make this money," Ishmael committed, eyeing Broderick closely.

TWO HOURS AFTER THE MEETING, Broderick sat in the front seat of Malcolm's limo as the driver rode through the streets, heading to a local mom and pop restaurant. Broderick continued looking out the window as the car turned down a familiar street.

"My men don't trust you."

"Your job is to get them to trust me," Broderick replied, expressionless and steadily looking forward.

Malcolm chuckled.

"This isn't a bad area; the Bronx is home. We take care of each other."

"Taking care means bringing guns and drugs around."

"Touché."

The driver stopped in front of Eloise's. Everyone knew

this was the clear zone; nothing happened when you stepped through those doors out of respect for the couple and the family that built the restaurant over fifty years ago. Currently run by the grandchildren and close friend of Malcolm, Jersey Hanson, a woman who was interested in more than a one-night stand. Broderick and Malcolm stepped out of the car, with more security following behind as they marched inside, nodding at the hostess and knowing who they came to meet. Broderick held his hand out, halting Malcolm's steps.

"Remember we need Maksim to trust you."

"Obviously, I'm in this to make sure my people don't get harmed," Malcolm spat back, treading to the table of men sitting down.

"Keep it that way," Broderick reminded, following toward the crowd of security standing around the table. During the afternoon hour, they closed the place down for private conversations between mafia families.

"Mr. Holmes, finally we've set something up," Maksim's second lieutenant said.

"Where's Maksim?" Malcolm asked, staring at two men sitting with four bodyguards behind them; neither one looked like Maksim Petrov. It was eerily silent for a few minutes as all men wanted to come across as the top boss throughout the entire meeting, but Broderick studied each man and kept his shades on, while Gregory captured the camera footage back in the Agency.

"Maksim will make contact soon, but for now, we come with good news," Saveli said, giving Broderick a long look.

"Do I know you?" Saveli chucked his chin up at Broderick.

"He doesn't speak," Malcolm said.

"You have them trained well." Saveli grinned.

Broderick clenched his teeth in aggravation.

"I'm open to giving Maksim five percent of gambling business."

"We were thinking fifty," Saveli remarked, leaning back in the chair.

"That'll never happen." Malcolm started to rise out of his seat.

Saveli held his hand up, stopping him from leaving.

"Twenty percent?" Saveli asked.

"Five percent, and that's me being generous. Before we start, let's be clear. I run everything here. Won't get out of hand, Saveli." Malcolm leaned forward, peering into Saveli's eyes.

Saveli' held his hands up in surrender.

"No problem, that's what you Americans say, right?" Saveli clenched his hands, leaning forward on the table.

"As long as we understand where things stand."

"The guns?" Saveli inquired.

"What are your plans for the guns? I heard your boss has a lot of issues."

"What issues?"

Malcolm shrugged.

"His name is on the streets over some agent getting shot," Malcolm brought up.

"We've not heard of this before." Saveli curled his lip up.

"So you have no clue about the police looking for your family?"

"None, but we know how your name is always run around here."

"I can handle my business, but I'm not getting my people sucked into some international bullshit." Malcolm narrowed in frustration.

"I'll inform Maksim of your concerns, but we'd like to move forward."

Malcolm nodded.

"Set up a meeting with Maksim, and I'll see about agreeing." Malcolm stood straight up, never leaving the Petrov family to stew if they'd have to make an example out of Malcolm Holmes. All the men stalked back to the car, heading back to the warehouse to reconvene. Malcolm didn't ask any questions as they arrived back to their cars at the warehouse, and Broderick hurriedly jumped out. Watching as he got into his car, Malcolm was slightly impressed that Broderick wasn't trying to demand any more information from the meeting and let him lead.

TWENTY MINUTES LATER, Broderick pulled up to the security garage in the back of the building, waiting to be approved for entrance. Something that had been playing over in his head made him think that Maksim was closer to them in the city, maybe even watching as they talked. Saveli kept his eyes focused on him rather than Malcolm, causing the hairs on the back of his neck to rise. He rubbed a hand down his face as the garage door opened, allowing him to park in the usual spot. Climbing out, Broderick nodded at another soldier coming out of the elevator. He stepped on and hit the floor for his team. The low music of jazz playing kept his mind clear and intent on what needed to happen.

"I need a life," Broderick mumbled to himself, stepping off the elevator a few minutes later.

Strolling down the hallway, Broderick appeared in front of Teagan's door and knocked.

"Come in!" she called out.

Pushing the door open, he was waved in to sit down as the TV played in the background on CNN.

"Any updates?" Teagan sat back, crossing her legs, tapping her middle and index fingers on the desk.

"I had a meeting with Saveli."

Teagan's eyes rose in surprise.

"What about Maksim?"

"My guess is he's either still out of the country or watching from a distance."

"You suspect he was there, not showing his face?"

"Yeah, it just felt off, and Saveli specifically asked if he knew me."

"What did Malcolm say?"

"He kept the conversation about the gambling fee and guns."

"Is he signing off?" Teagan wondered.

"Yeah, but hesitant on guns."

"We need him to be all in on this, Broderick. Remind him of our deal."

"I will, and I got the footage for Gregory."

"Good. I believe Maksim is coming hard, and we need to be prepared."

"I agree. Are you going to meet with the president tomorrow?"

"Yeah, and I'm not looking forward to dealing with Duncan." Teagan blew out a breath.

"When do you fly out?" Broderick questioned.

"Early morning."

"Try not to get in the news again." Broderick rose out of his seat.

"Depends on if someone pisses me off."

FOUR

The next day, Teagan sat in the black Lincoln town car passing by the monuments she grew up hearing about. Now in her position, she had a bigger role to uphold the vision and principles of America that no one had the guts to do every day. She went out on missions never knowing if her husband and children would think this was the last moment of saying goodbye.

Flashback.

Teagan was bent over the toilet, throwing up last night's dinner that her parents cooked at her coming home party. She was one year back from her last mission, and CJ was just getting in the habit of talking. Cole was still a baby that Christian was raising while she was away. A knock on the bathroom door came, and she sat with her eyes closed, wondering how she would tell Christian she was going back out soon, and she was pregnant. Being happily married came with struggles, and one was fighting enemies who didn't care if she had a husband and child. She put herself in certain situations Christian may not forgive or forget.

"Honey, it's me, Mom." *Teagan crawled to the door and*

unlocked it, letting her mom come in and lock it behind her. Peering up, Teagan gave a brave smile.

"You have to go back."

Teagan nodded.

"Where?"

"I can't say."

"How long?"

"I don't know." Teagan adjusted to sit up against the counter.

"When you told me this was your plan of getting into the Navy, I was proud, but scared."

"Me too."

"You want to know what convinced me to be okay and not worry?"

"What?"

"You." She motioned at her.

"Me," Teagan said, surprised.

"Teagan, you're more of your father's temperament and presence, calm and focused. You never waver."

"I always feel like I struggle. I'm the only girl sometimes."

"Then take that thought and make it work for you. We all know what they think of women."

"So use it to my advantage?" she queried.

"Use it to guide you in life, not only missions, but your marriage and being a mother. Calm and focused," her mom reminded, running a hand down her cheek.

"Thanks."

"I'm excited for the new baby."

Teagan chuckled as her mom winked and left her to her thoughts.

Present.

"We're here, ma'am," Sean said, opening the passenger

side door as Teagan got out wearing a long, black trench coat, covering a black Chanel pants suit and black heels with her hair hanging down in curls. Taking the same advice her mom told her years ago, she was calm and focused, knowing Duncan would try to rattle her.

"Thank you, Sean," Teagan said, grabbing her briefcase and purse out of the backseat.

Going through security, Teagan raised her arms up as the wand went across her shoulders, under her arms, down to the sides. She already had an appointment scheduled, and everyone knew who she was from all the media hype of her past arrest.

"Free to go," the security guard said.

"Thank you."

Teagan met up with the chief of staff standing a few feet away at Noah Anderson, an ally of The Firm, and keeping the president updated at all times. Some people came and went, but Noah was the most loyal when she needed something from the president.

"Teagan, thanks for coming," Noah said, holding his hand out for her to continue journeying.

"Thanks for setting this up."

"Well, the minute your budget gets approved, the president wants to stay in touch."

"Even though my face has been plastered all over the world?" she questioned.

"Yep." Noah chuckled with his boyish looks. Not even hitting forty years old, he sat next to the most powerful man in the world. Noah's six-three with low cut, smooth black hair, wide shoulders, grey eyes, and full nose.

"Before we go inside, I have to tell you Duncan is here."

"I figured he'd make an appearance."

"The president wants to make sure things run smoothly."

"I have no plans of stooping to his level."

"Another thing is that afterwards, reporters will come in for photos."

"I didn't know we'd have a photo shoot today."

"The administration thought having you two together would signal all parties can work together."

"I'm not a politician, Noah."

"I agree, but you get more out of the situation and let Duncan fold under the pressure." Noah pushed the door open. Strolling in, Teagan saw the president and Duncan sitting as she smiled with her hand held out for a handshake.

"Mr. President." Teagan extended her palm, and he grasped it.

"Teagan, thank you for coming. I know it's been awhile," President Sanders remarked.

Teagan let out a low breath, turning toward Duncan as he stood to shake her hand.

"Duncan."

"Agent Stone." Duncan sat back on the individual chair as Teagan and Noah took a seat on the couch.

"I called this meeting because we need to align with the vision," President Sanders stated.

"Yes, sir."

"Did I not approve the budget?" Duncan remarked.

"As you did, it came with a little bit of a show," Teagan reminded him.

"Well, I need the American people to know where their tax money is going."

"Noah, do you want to talk?" President Sanders nudged him to dive into the conversation.

"As the president was saying, the current focus is on Maksim Petrov," Noah said. Teagan quickly looked at Duncan for any hints of him working with Maksim.

"Being on the national security committee, we've run across his file," Duncan called out.

Noah placed photos of Maksim on the table.

"What do we know so far?" Noah asked Teagan.

"He's planning something. What? I don't know. My team is working around the clock."

"If you don't have anything on him, why are we wasting money on a lost cause?" Duncan asked.

Teagan had a talent for knowing when bullshit was spraying out of someone's mouth, and Duncan was falling right into her hands.

"It's never a waste to protect American people."

"So, are we saying this man is planning an attack?" Duncan pointed at the photo of Maksim.

"I'm saying it's better to be over-cautious than under."

"Have you run across any information, Duncan, that tells us we shouldn't?" President Sanders questioned.

"Not much beside the usual."

"Really? We have a lot of information from the security council." Teagan opened her briefcase and pulled out a thick file on Maksim.

President Sanders watched as Duncan squirmed in his seat, loosening his tie.

"You must have gotten new information from the past few months. Or year."

"Must have," Teagan replied, opening the file and passing around text messages and phone call information around the room.

"These are travel dates and text messages he's been

engaged in for the last few weeks," Teagan stated. Duncan's gaze never left hers as she grabbed more evidence.

"I think we need to stay on the investigation."

"We should be focused on what we know is harmful to our security, and that's China and Iran," Duncan huffed, tossing the papers back down on the table.

Teagan, Noah, and President Sanders all glanced at each other after his outburst.

"I have trust that Teagan and the team can multitask," President Sanders said.

"Don't say anything now, but it's on your shoulders following an end ride," Duncan said.

Teagan felt Duncan didn't have to be an asshole or make it seem like the work they were doing had been around for generations of presidents.

"Mr. President." Julie popped her head inside.

The president's secretary carried a piece of paper over to him to read.

"I need to take this call. Do you mind if we end our meeting early?" the president stated as he stood and extended his hand to Duncan, then to Teagan.

"I'll be here for another few hours, sir, if you need anything," Teagan said, bending down to grab the file folder with Maksim's information. Noah escorted her and Duncan out of the office. Duncan held his cell phone out, sending a text message, as Teagan watched from the side, listening to Noah explain the president's upcoming schedule.

"He's flying to Canada for two days," Noah replied.

"Huh."

"I said, the president will get to you once he's back from his visits," Noah explained. Teagan watched as Duncan's face furrowed in a harsh grimace. A few seconds went by, and he ran a sideways glance toward Teagan and Noah and hurriedly stomped away.

Noah shook his head as he continued to escort Teagan out of the White House.

"Someone's in a hurry," Noah muttered, pushing the door open on the west side as Sean stood.

"I agree with you." Teagan stared as Duncan's car pulled off soon as he entered.

"Well, I'll let you get back to your duties."

Teagan shook hands with Noah and nodded. Getting in the car, the door shut, and Sean walked around to the driver's side.

"Follow that car!"

"Yes, ma'am," Sean replied.

Teagan lifted her cell out of her purse, looking for Gregory's message thread.

Gregory: I have the video footage.

Teagan: I need you to trace something.

Sean pushed through traffic one car behind Duncan's limo.

Gregory: Who is it?

Teagan: Congressman Duncan... FN-456

Gregory: Typing it in now.

Driving through three lights, the car stopped finally in front of a coffee shop, and Duncan jumped out and rushed inside.

"Should I park, ma'am?"

"No, let's wait a minute."

Less than five minutes later, he came out with a coffee and a white package under his arm. Getting back in the car, they drove off again through main streets and arriving at the Capitol. Teagan held her cell phone up, taking pictures of

Duncan hiking up the steps, drinking whatever he ordered, and holding on tight to the envelope.

Gregory: Registered to Duncan personally.

Teagan: He made another stop before heading to the Capitol.

Gregory: Was he meeting anyone?

Teagan: I don't know, but he left with an envelope.

Gregory: What's the address?

Teagan: Berry's Coffee and Bagel.

Gregory: I'll see if they have cameras and get back to you.

Teagan: Thanks, Gregory.

"We can go back to the hotel."

Closing out of the message thread, Sean left, driving at a fast speed when the whirling lights of the police came up behind them. Teagan looked through the back window, pursing her lips together, curious as to why they were getting pulled over.

"First time I've ever gotten a ticket," Sean called out.

He turned his signal light on and slowed to the right side out of Main Street.

"It shouldn't take too long," Teagan said.

A minute went by, then a knock on the window came, and a police officer leaned into the window.

"License and registration," the officer asked.

"Why was I stopped?" Sean asked.

Teagan stared at the officer as he continued talking with Sean, holding onto her phone with the video low, filming him. Sean passed his license over.

"Speeding. What is your business in DC?" he questioned.

"What makes you think we don't live here?" Teagan brought up.

His eyes scanned to the backseat. She watched as the arrogant, cocky demeanor disappeared.

"Based on your speeding, and I'm asking the questions here."

"Of course."

"Do you have any drugs or anything I need to know?"

"No," Sean answered.

Listening to the bullshit come out of his mouth made it obvious that Duncan called in a favor.

"If we aren't getting a ticket, can we go now?" Teagan said.

She watched as his lip curled in disgust.

"Keep an eye on your speeding, and you're free to go," the officer stated, passing the license and registration back before turning back to his car.

"That was strange," Sean said.

"No, that was a warning," Teagan said, watching the police car speed by them as they headed to the hotel for the rest of the day.

A FEW HOURS LATER, Teagan was showered, sitting in her hotel bed on her laptop, eating the pasta she'd ordered from room service. With a Diet Coke on the nightstand, she stared at every angle of the video clip of Broderick's meeting with Malcolm and Maksim's people. Gregory sent everything as soon as he'd finished organizing and timestamping. Getting files on Saveli and Nail was just as hard on Maksim. These men had hands in high places and possibly the police force. That little stunt of getting pulled over to scare her caused a chuckle now. Earlier, it was a moment she didn't know if she'd have to throw her weight around and let him know that Duncan couldn't save him if he continued to pursue this fake speeding ticket.

The next file emailed to her contained still photos of Duncan heading into Berry's shop like a normal customer would and ordering a drink at the counter. He then went out of frame, more than likely to the bathrooms. Gregory didn't have a camera visual of that back area, so all Teagan could go with was the visual of him coming back into frame with something under his arm as he grabbed the drink from the counter.

"What are you hiding, Duncan?"

Ring

Ring

Taking her phone off the charger, she saw Christian's name pop up. Checking the time, she answered, "Hey."

"Did I catch you at a bad time?" Christian asked.

"No, just relaxing and going through some paperwork."

"The kids miss you and are ready for you to come home."

"I miss them and you."

"Did the meeting go well?" Christian always changed the subject when she got to talking about missing him. In his mind, he didn't understand why she took so many cases out of state. Being the director should come with letting other people handle those jobs.

"It did."

"What did you eat for dinner?"

"My favorite pasta and Italian bread," Teagan chortled, hearing Christian laughing on the other end of the phone.

"I won't hold you up any longer. I'll see you tomorrow," Christian said.

"Love you."

"Love you more," he responded, hanging up the phone.

FIVE

Three weeks later.

Sliding into the seat across from Spider, Teagan looked around the restaurant and lifted the chai latte to her lips to take a sip. Feeling the sweet nectar to her lips filled her mind and gave her a burst of energy. Since she came back to the city, she'd been home taking care of the kids and being a wife. Tatum was sick, and CJ had a few games, so she cut back on work and left Spider in charge unless it was an emergency. Now that Christian was full time as well, bringing in a nanny was an entire new job as they held interviews. Spider knew what her favorite drinks and food were just as much as Christian and made great conversations on missions.

"Thanks for ordering ahead for me," Teagan said.

The waitress walked over to their table, placing a veggie omelet, sausages, eggs, fruit, and a waffle down, along with ketchup and utensils.

"No problem. I figured you'd be ready to dive in at your favorite place."

"This is your favorite place. I just deal with the

outcome." Spider worked out and had a great physique but ate horribly, especially when it came to carbs.   They'd argued many times on healthy eating. Teagan tried to get him to include more veggies, but it never worked.

"How's the family doing?" Spider questioned.

"Family is good. Christian is great."

"Did you guys find a nanny yet?" Spider poured ketchup on his hash browns.

"Not yet. Tatum just got over a cold."

"Did you give her the doll I got?"

"Yes, and she's more than spoiled thanks to you."

"My pleasure."

"Anyway, tell me how Broderick is doing?" Teagan questioned.

"They had a few gambling nights, and he's gotten footage."

Teagan cut into her omelet and took a bite, closing her eyes and moaning over the spices mixed together. Letting the steam from her tea simmer, she lifted it up and blew over the top.

"Did Gregory go through the footage?"

Spider nodded in answer. "He's still going through everything and checking over the guests in attendance."

"Has Malcolm said anything?"

"No, we keep our end of the bargain, and he'll be fine."

"You think we can bring him down?"

"Congressman Duncan? Yeah, he's going to fuck up, and we'll catch him."

Teagan leaned on the table with her hand on her head.

"Maksim is here in New York. I can feel it in my blood."

"He can't run too far without us finding out," Spider answered.

An hour into their conversation, the waitress checked in and refilled their drinks.

"Anything else I can get for you two?" Stephanie smiled, picking up the empty plates and leaving the check.

"No, everything was fine." Teagan laid her knife and fork down, wiping her mouth clean. She peered down at her phone ringing, with Gregory's name showing. She picked it up as they stood from their booth.

"Hello," Teagan said.

Spider gestured for her to walk ahead, leaving to go back to the office.

"Teagan, I wanted to update you on what I found," Gregory mentioned. Teagan headed to her security detail as Spider hopped into his car.

"Please let it be good news."

"I have Duncan's offshore account unlocked," Gregory said.

"On my way," Teagan replied, ending the call.

Thirty minutes later, Teagan and Spider walked into the conference room as Gregory and Daughtrey sat around talking. Teagan removed her jacket, placing it on the back of her chair, and sat at the head of the table.

"Let's hear the news."

Gregory held his laptop in front of him, turning it around to show Teagan and Spider.

"Joshua Kline."

"Who is this?" Spider asked.

"Remember that phone call Teagan got a few weeks ago that I couldn't trace?"

Teagan and Spider nodded. "Based on Duncan's phone records, I was able to figure out who he's been communicating with."

"Does it lead back to this guy?" Spider queried, holding a picture of Joshua from social media.

"Any criminal records?"

"Nothing so far. I just was able to start researching before I called you."

Daughtrey tossed a crumbled paper in a ball up in the air.

"What are you thinking, Teagan?" Daughtrey wondered.

Teagan pushed the photo back, crossing her arms over her chest.

"What's the motive for Joshua and Duncan to work together?"

"Money," everyone answered at the same time.

"We can't bring this to Duncan without backup; he might go into hiding."

"The president needs to know about this update," Spider said, picking up the photo.

"I'm not so sure. We still have Maksim missing."

"I agree. Why bring down one when we can catch all the players?" Daughtrey glanced over at them.

"Malcolm and Broderick are still working at Maksim. I need to get as much evidence as possible."

"Am I the only one who's thinking of a potential attack? We knew ahead of time and did nothing," Spider fussed.

"Look, the second I bring this up, and it leaks to the press, all of our jobs are on the line," Teagan responded, motioning to the photo.

"So, we just sit and wait!" Spider threw his hands in the air, exasperated.

"That's my final decision, whether you agree or not." Teagan arched her brow at Spider.

"When are we checking in with Broderick?" Daughtrey asked.

"He should be getting us updates by tomorrow." Teagan checked her watch and stood.

Spider sighed and ran a hand down his face in frustration.

"I have CJ's football game this weekend. Spider, follow up with Gregory. We don't move on Joshua yet. Daughtrey, check in with Broderick. Keep me updated," Teagan said, leaving for the evening.

"You think she's making the wrong decision?" Daughtrey questioned.

"What if they get a hold of a bomb and something happens?" Spider whistled.

"Teagan hasn't been wrong since she came back," Gregory admitted, scratching the back of his neck.

"Let's hope she continues with that streak," Spider muttered as he pushed the door open and left for his office.

ACROSS TOWN LATER THAT NIGHT, Broderick stood on the main floor of Malcolm's business that he used for a gambling ring, watching for any sign of Maksim Petrov. What he didn't know was that Maksim had eyes on what was happening while he was at the warehouse meeting to finalize his plans. Soon as the money dropped into Malcolm's account, he allowed some of his property to be used, even though he kept this from Broderick and Teagan. He felt it was best to limit the amount of interaction of Maksim coming and going at his main location of funneling money.

The cigar smoke filled the room, and each person sat in

unison, waiting on their boss to speak. They knew when orders were given out, they would obey without hesitation. That concept was lost on Duncan Brooks when he received a text message that since police and FBI were sniffing around, the final deposit wouldn't arrive. Maksim planned each moment to perfection. To his surprise, Duncan demanded a meeting with him.

"Speak," Maksim stated, blowing smoke in Duncan's face. A round table at Malcolm's warehouse was used at the last minute; it was in a neutral place that looked like a normal business on the outside. As Congressman, he was running on thin ice, not only in his party with getting certain bills passed, but he was also dealing with a divorce and a pill problem. He only wanted to get his five million and leave the country.

"Maksim, we both agreed that my part in this was limited," Duncan spat, rubbing his temple.

Maksim grinned, placing the cigar in the ashtray. "Mr. Congressman, have I not paid you well?" Maksim cracked his knuckles.

"You've only paid me half," Duncan answered.

"Nail, bring Mr. Congressman a drink. He's looking thirsty."

"I'm fine. I don't need anything."

"Are you refusing to drink with me? Am I not good enough for the big congressman?" Maksim joked, his men laughing along with him.

Nail leaned over the conference table, taking the glass of cognac, and poured a shot for each man. Standing, he passed the drink over to Maksim, then Duncan. Lifting it to his lips, Maksim stared into Duncan's eyes as he gulped the drink down.

"Ahhh... refreshing," Maksim said, grabbing the cigar again.

"Again, I wanted to meet because I need my other half," Duncan pleaded.

"What money?" Maksim snorted.

"I put my life on the line for you," Duncan hissed, pointing his finger at Maksim.

"Mr. Brooks, I think it's best you understand who you're speaking with."

Maksim stood from his seat, sliding his hands in his pockets, and walked over to the mirror hanging on the wall. He looked over his shoulder, winked at Duncan, and turned the switch on the wall. The window turned into a TV monitor with Duncan's soon to be ex-wife on the screen. She was standing in the kitchen, cooking.

Duncan spat out his drink, trying to jump up, but Nail held him down by the shoulders, placing a knife under his neck.

"Please, she has nothing to do with this," Duncan argued.

"You think so?"

Maksim chucked his head to the left for Nail to let Duncan go.

"Okay, I get the message," Duncan said.

"Once Joshua completes what I need, then you might get your money," Maksim told him.

"What about Teagan Stone?"

"That's your problem."

"She's onto you. I don't know how, but she has the backing of the president."

"I suggest you handle her or else she will handle you."

"Maksim."

Maksim lifted his index finger to stop him.

"You should have known things wouldn't work out for you."

Duncan rushed out of the warehouse, scrambling for his cell phone out of his pocket. Feeling like he may have bitten off more than he could handle, he dialed his wife, even though they were no longer together.

The phone rang three times with no answer.

"Pick up, goddamn it!" he growled, rubbing the back of his head. He ended the call and dialed again.

"You have reached my voicemail," Cheryl's voice recording stated.

"Fuck!" Duncan shouted, tucking the phone back in his pocket before removing his keys. He stalked to his car. Stepping off the curb, he slid the key into the door but when he heard footsteps behind him, he stuck his hand in his pocket, pretending it was a gun.

"Don't move!" he yelled.

"Congressman, it's me," Sandra spoke.

Duncan looked startled but slowly relaxed once he recognized her from TV.

"Sandra Gregg from GHS News."

"I was hoping to speak with you."

"At this time of night, eight thirty?"

"The story never sleeps," Sandra replied cockily.

"Sorry, I don't talk to reporters."

"You sure about that?" She cocked her head to the side.

"Whatever you think you know, I'll have my attorneys bury it by the morning."

"I never said I had anything, sir."

"Let it stay that way." Duncan started to slide into his car.

"The story could be me seeing suspicious activity at a warehouse."

Duncan removed his keys, jumping back out of the car.

"Are you crazy! Do you know who owns this building?" Duncan pointed.

"I do. Malcolm Holmes, a local gun and illegal gambling ringleader."

"Exactly, so tread very carefully, Miss Gregg."

"I will, and I'd say the same for you," Sandra said, walking away as Duncan got in his car again and drove off. Sandra headed to the back corner of the building where she left her car. She removed the tape recorder and pressed rewind. Listening to the playback, she smiled at possibly breaking a story with the local congressman and drug dealer. As she did this, Maksim watched from above the warehouse and smirked at more rats interfering in his game. The idea of bringing more destruction in the country gave him an excitement he loved to chase.

SIX

Malcolm walked around his establishment as loud grumbles and excitement whirled around from customers winning and losing. He'd set this illegal casino to hold deals on the side with his gun business, starting out small with a few men in attendance until it grew from word of mouth. Now, criminals from all over the world showed up just to see what he offered for entertainment. A few of his men came tonight to relax and party with the strippers. Mr. Holmes stayed clean from any alcohol so he could stay focused and alert. He'd just gotten a text message that Maksim ended his meeting and left the warehouse, so he could chill slightly. He walked toward his office with Broderick, and two more bodyguards followed behind. Unlocking the door with his key, he stepped around his desk, removing his jacket and unbuttoning his shirt. Picking the phone up off the desk, he dialed to the girls' room he had built.

"This is Bambi," she said, making him grow harder in his pants. Over the past few weeks, he hadn't spent any time with her, and he knew she'd be pissed, so he tried to ease into the conversation.

"Come to my office."

"I'm busy," she answered.

"I didn't ask what you were doing."

"Malcolm," she mumbled.

"Please come to my office. I have a surprise," Malcolm responded, ending the call.

Tonya Johnson, better known as Bambi, was twenty-five years old, slim, mahogany-brown skin, five-five, full lips, high cheekbones, and a smile that lit up a room and caused every man to give her anything she desired. Currently in college to be a nurse and working part time for Malcolm as a stripper, she never expected to fall for her boss, but one night they were working late, and he offered to give her a ride home. Ever since then, she'd been his only companion. Hearing a knock on the door, he pressed the button underneath his desk, and she walked inside wearing a robe and high heels.

"Yes, you summoned me," Bambi spat, crossing her arms over her chest.

"I missed you."

"Malcolm."

"All right, come here." He reached out for her hand, and she rolled her eyes and came around his desk, allowing him to pull her onto his lap. Wrapping his arm around her waist, he squeezed her close and kissed the top of her shoulder.

"How are you?" he asked.

"Fine."

"How's school?"

"Fine."

"Really, Tonya?"

She tried to get up from his lap, but he tightened his hold.

"What do you want from me?" she questioned.

"I apologize for not staying in touch; I've been busy," Malcolm begged.

"No, you've ignored me."

Malcolm ran a hand up and down her arm.

"Work has been crazy."

"Are you still doing the deal with that Russian guy?" Bambi asked.

"I can't talk about that."

"You can't or won't?" she fussed.

"It's complicated."

"Do you know who this man is? The things he's done."

"I never said I was a saint, baby."

"You lie down with dogs, you end up getting fleas."

"I'm working with the government," Malcolm muttered.

She turned her body to sit sideways in his lap.

"What did you say?"

"Just know that I'm being protected."

"Okay." Bambi caressed his cheek.

"Okay what?"

"I'll leave it alone for now, but I refuse to put my life on the line," Bambi informed him.

Malcolm gripped the back of her neck and met her halfway for a kiss.

"Are you hungry?" Malcolm inquired, running his lips down her cheek toward the back of her neck.

"Yeah, I didn't eat much during class."

"Well, let me order you something."

"You're not working the floor tonight?"

Malcolm shook his head no.

"I have enough men. I can stay back for now."

"So, I have you all to myself tonight."

Bambi rubbed up and down his chest.

"Anything in particular you want to do?" Malcolm placed the phone back down as Bambi giggled.

"I can think of a few things." Bambi chuckled when Malcolm lifted her off his lap, planting her on top of the desk.

THE WEEKEND ARRIVED, and Abby Kline tried once again to call and check up on her brother Joshua. The kids were in the backyard playing around as she sat with her computer, reviewing news articles and information on Maksim Petrov. After living that vague phone call with Dr. Stone, she wanted to potentially go to the police, but she was scared of what could happen to her family if it ever got out that she'd gone snooping around.

"Mommy, come play," her daughter announced, running up on her holding a doll in her hands.

"Okay, baby. Give me one minute." Abby listened as the voice message continued. She sighed, closing her eyes and feeling defeated.

"Hey, babe." Her husband bent down and kissed the back of her neck. She quickly closed her computer.

"Are you all right? Did I scare you or something?" He sat on the opposite end of the table, picking his daughter up in his lap.

"Huh?"

"What's going on? You seem distracted," Courtland wondered.

"No, I'm fine."

"Is it Josh? Babe, he's an adult," her husband stated, not knowing what was really going on with the family.

"How was work this week?" Abby changed the subject.

"Work was work. Same thing as always."

"Did you make the sale?"

He nodded in answer.

"Great, so you're home for a week, right?"

He brushed the top of his daughter's head with his palm. "No, I have to fly out in two days."

Abby stood, grabbing her daughter from her husband's lap and walking toward the swing set.

"Abby... Abby, let's not fight."

She quickly pivoted around.

"No, you're never home anymore. I feel—" She stopped, realizing she was still holding her daughter in her arms.

"Baby, go play with your brother," Abby said.

"Once this trip is done, I'll take a vacation." He closed the gap between them, wrapping his arms around her waist.

"You say that every time."

"How do you think we live in this big house and send our kids to private school?"

"Here you go with throwing your money in my face." Abby pushed him back, stomping back to the porch.

"Would you stop acting like a child!" Courtland shouted.

"Mommy! Daddy! Stop fighting!" their daughter screamed.

Abby wiped her face clear of tears and turned around, smiling.

"Honey, everything is fine. Daddy and I are just talking," Abby explained.

"Yeah, sweetheart. Keep swinging, and I'll be over there soon," he said.

"See what you made me do!" Abby hissed slowly.

"If you stop all this nonsense with your brother," Courtland argued.

She cut him off with her hand up.

"Don't talk about my brother. This has everything to do with you constantly working."

Throwing his hands in the air, he blew out an aggravated breath.

"All I'm trying to do is provide for my family, Abby."

"Which I get, but you're away more than you used to be in the beginning."

"Because as the top sales rep, they need me more."

"Whatever."

"How about we have a nice dinner tonight and send the kids to my brother's house?"

"I guess."

He pecked her lips.

"Great, I'll give him a call and make the reservations. You get the kids packed."

SANDRA GREGG SHUT her computer down and grabbed her purse and keys. The only time she worked the weekends was during a big case, and she wanted to do more research on the warehouse Duncan was at the other night. Waving goodbye to her coworkers, she left the GHS news station. In the employee parking lot, Sandra tossed her things inside her car and slid the key into the ignition, turning on her favorite country station to the sound of Garth Brooks. She swayed her head to the music, mumbling the lyrics slowly as she pulled into traffic. This was her big breakout moment and if Maksim were brought down with her name on the article, her dream of being on the major network morning shows would catapult her to stardom. The sweltering heat in New York, and an increase in traffic, made her slow down, opening the top button of her shirt and fanning herself. Lifting her shades, she looked out the windows at the cars next to her, playing loud music. The two young men, with short, black hair, grey eyes, and olive skin tone, sitting in the BMW, looked younger than she'd date, but they were cute. One looked over at her with an evil grin on his face, pretending his finger was a gun. The car drove off before they could hear her statement.

"Asshole!" she yelled, throwing up the middle finger.

Hearing a car honking behind her, she turned into the right lane and drove on, shaking her head at the idiot drivers. Continuing on her journey, she came upon another traffic buildup five minutes later and cursed under her breath for going the long way home today. Noticing no cars moving, she looked left to right in her side mirror and saw the same car from earlier two cars behind. The passenger stared right back toward her car. Not paying too much attention, she checked the time and saw after three cars passed the four-way light on Avenue and Broadway was out.

"Just my luck." She sucked her teeth.

Letting one car go from the left, she waited, then took her turn. As she almost passed, another car drove through on the right side, almost hitting her car if she didn't speed up.

"Oh my God!" She tried getting a better handle on the steering wheel and pulled off to the side, placing her car in park and closing her eyes as her heart beat rapidly. For a split second, she opened her eyes again, seeing the BMW pass her with the passenger blowing her a kiss.

SEVEN

Saturday

The sun beamed down on the football field as CJ ran after his opponent while Teagan, Tatum, and Cole screamed and cheered at him. While her mind was still very much on finding Maksim and getting Duncan arrested, Teagan had to carve out of her schedule moments of being a mom, going to football games, and wearing shirts with their school mascots on the back. Tatum wore a cheerleading outfit to feel like one of the girls out on the field. Christian meanwhile slept in since he worked overtime, so she packed a cooler with snacks and tablets to keep them preoccupied on the ride over.

"Yay! Let's go, CJ!" Teagan yelled out.

Teagan helped Tatum with her bottled water and picked one up for herself. Taking her phone out of her purse, she scrolled her messages and emails for any updates.

"Mommy, can we have pizza tonight?" Cole asked.

"Not tonight, baby. I have to cook. You've had pizza already this week."

"How about tacos?" Cole counteroffered.

Teagan laughed, shaking her head.

"Another time, Cole."

"How much longer, Mommy? I want to go shopping," Tatum said.

"Baby, not much longer. Look at your brother." Teagan motioned, putting her phone back in her pocket.

"He has the ball. Go CJ!" Tatum jumped up and down, spilling her water.

The referee blew the whistle, and everyone ran to their team sections to regroup. CJ walked over to his mom, removing his helmet.

"Good job, baby." Teagan kissed the side of his cheek, wiping it off right after knowing he hated when she embarrassed him.

"Thanks, Mom. Can I go over to Kenny's house after this is over?" CJ asked, holding his hands together in prayer. Teagan hated being the bad guy, but after finding out one of her close friends was an enemy, she kept her kids from being around other families. She didn't mind the children coming to her house, but in her line of work, she couldn't trust anyone.

"Kenny can come to our house, but no more sleepovers, baby."

CJ nodded in agreement.

"Great, let me head back out, and I'll tell him." CJ placed his helmet back on and ran to the field.

Feeling vibration, Teagan reached in her pocket and took out her phone, seeing a message from Broderick.

Teagan: I'm free.

Broderick: We got the word Maksim is here.

Teagan: How do you know?

Broderick: He contacted Duncan.

Teagan: What did Malcolm say?

Broderick: He pulled the footage from inside the warehouse.

Teagan closed the messages and dialed Broderick's number, stepping a few feet away from the kids sitting on the benches.

"Who was in the room?"

"Duncan, Maksim, Saveli, and more of his men."

"Malcolm wasn't there?"

"No, and I was pissed."

"How did that happen?"

"He had all his men at the casino."

"So he happened to just give you the footage?"

"I heard him talking with one of the strippers he's dating."

Teagan continued to stare at her kids watching the game.

"Did he say why we weren't informed about this meeting?"

"Some vague answer about running things his way."

"Bring him to the office." Teagan ended the call, walking back over to her children.

"Mommy, we won! We won!" Tatum screamed up and down.

"I see, baby. Let's grab our things so we can be ready to leave. Mommy has to make a stop before we go home," Teagan said, hating that she had to bring her kids to work, but this was time sensitive. Letting Malcolm feel like he was in charge would no longer work for her. Packing up their items, the crowd dispersed as the team enjoyed winning another game for their school. CJ ran over with Kenny behind him and his parents.

"Kenny told us you okayed for him to hang out with CJ this afternoon," Kenny's mom said.

"Yes, if you're okay with that. I can give you my phone number and my husband's," Teagan said, walking to her car.

Stacy took her phone from her purse and listened to Teagan rattle off her number.

"Kenny, be good for Mrs. Hawkins." Stacy took some of his equipment from his hands.

"I will, Mom," Kenny answered. Teagan opened the backseat and walked to the trunk to put the rest of the bags and the cooler inside.

Helping Tatum and Cole in their seats, she closed the door and hopped into the driver's side. Teagan turned the music up in the car, keeping the kids preoccupied as she sent a message to Christian on her phone.

Teagan: Babe, I need you to come get the kids.

Christian: What's going on? How's the game?

Teagan: They won, but I need to head to the office.

Christian: Teagan, really? It's Saturday.

Teagan: I know, but it's closer to my office.

Christian: You know how I feel about having them near that place.

Teagan: I'm going to have security watch them.

Christian: I'm on my way.

Teagan: Sorry.

Making it to her destination, she pulled up to the entrance, and security checked her ID before the guard gate opened.

"Mommy, where are we?" Tatum questioned.

"I needed to get something from the office, baby."

"Ooh, can I see your office?" Tatum asked.

"Not this time." Getting the green light to come inside, she pulled forward, turning into her reserved spot. Releasing a long-held breath, she looked at the kids through the rearview mirror as they admired all the cars, vans, and military trucks.

"Mom," CJ called out.

"Honey, I need you guys to stay here with my friend Sean."

Teagan finished texting Sean to come downstairs and placed the phone in her pocket. A few seconds later, Sean came around the corner of the elevator and met her behind the car.

"Are they up there?" she asked.

"Yes, ma'am."

"Good, watch my kids. I called Christian, and he's pissed."

"Do you want me to drive them home?" Sean asked.

Biting her bottom lip, she thought about it. Christian would probably be more aggravated if he dropped them off.

"No, they're fine waiting for him. Here are the keys."

"Do they need food?" Sean questioned.

"They're not dogs, Sean. They can tell you what they need." She walked off as he smirked at her statement.

***

ROLLING UP HER SLEEVES, Teagan strolled off to the elevator, focused on the target in her office. Sliding her key inside, she pushed the door open, glancing around the room. Broderick, Malcolm, and Spider were waiting quietly.

"Who do you think you are?" Teagan demanded, slamming her door, marching toward Malcolm, who sat in the chair in front of her desk. Spider and Broderick stood on either side of him.

"I made a mistake," Malcolm admitted.

"You made a mistake." Teagan tapped the side of her forehead.

"It won't happen again."

"Do you think we're a joke?" Teagan sat on the corner of her desk with her arms crossed.

"Listen, it won't happen again. I miscalculated," Malcolm said, looking forward at the wall of pictures.

"Mr. Holmes, this business, as you know, can be dangerous."

"What if we put a tail on him for twenty-four hours?" Broderick suggested, glaring at Malcolm.

"That won't be necessary," Malcolm responded.

Teagan shook her head, slamming her hand on the desk, eyes burning with irritation.

"You don't get to tell me or my team what is necessary."

Malcolm cleared his throat.

"How is Bambi doing?"

Malcolm's eyes rose in surprise.

"Leave her out of this," Malcolm responded.

"We got your attention now."

"He'll start a war if he finds out what I've done," Malcolm shouted.

"You won't even live long enough to see a war if you keep playing me." Teagan rose from the desk, walking around to her chair. She closed and opened her eyes a few minutes later in thought.

"Go forward with anything having to do with business, my people will know," Teagan rattled off. Malcolm interrupted, and she arched a brow.

"I want Maksim Petrov, but I'll take you down for shits and giggles if you try me again," Teagan explained, chucking her head toward the door for him to leave. Broderick left with him while Spider stayed behind.

"Think it'll work?" Spider asked.

"At this point, we have no choice."

"How was the football game?" Spider questioned, and Teagan tensed.

"Fuck!" She remembered the kids being downstairs with Sean. Grabbing her phone quickly, she dialed Christian's number.

"What's wrong?" Spider asked, following her out of the office.

"I forgot the kids downstairs." Teagan ran toward the stairs, not waiting for the elevator.

She made it to the garage, and her van was gone. Sean was talking with a coworker.

"Sean, where's the kids?" she asked.

"Your husband picked them up," Sean remarked.

Teagan relaxed, releasing a breath.

"Did he say anything?"

"Not really, just that he'll see you at home," Sean told him.

"You've never brought the kids here," Spider said.

"I know."

"I'll stay here and monitor for any updates."

"Are you sure?" Teagan replied.

Spider nodded.

"Go, you need to take a vacation anyway."

"That's been for a while. Let me get out of here," Teagan said.

Sean went over to the Lincoln town car they normally used to drive her around, opening the back passenger door. Teagan slid in and shut the door, placing her seatbelt on and trying to call Christian one more time.

THIRTY MINUTES LATER, Teagan waved good night to Sean as he pulled off, sliding the key into the front door of a dark, quiet house. Shutting and locking the door, she removed her jacket and kicked off her shoes.

Walking over to CJ's room, she peeked in and saw him sleeping under the covers. She headed to Tatum and Cole's rooms. Everyone was tucked in tight as she regretted missing another night with her kids. Slowly twisting the knob of her bedroom door, she pushed it open and strolled in quietly to find Christian sitting up watching a game on TV.

"You're still up?" Teagan said.

"Yeah."

Teagan went to sit on the edge of the bed, running a hand across Christian's leg in his shorts.

"When?" Christian turned the game off, placing the remote on the corner table.

"What do you mean?"

"When is it enough? Putting my kids in harm's way may not mean anything."

"Don't go there."

"No, let's go there." Christian jumped up out of bed.

"It's my job, Christian."

"No, it's your life, and I'm tired of the bullshit."

"Baby."

"There you go trying to be manipulative."

"Really, Christian, manipulative?" Teagan rolled her eyes and walked toward her dresser to grab her nightgown before heading to the bathroom.

"Yes, manipulative and acting like this is normal."

"I'm not in the mood to fight. It's been a long day." She picked up the toothbrush and paste, preparing for bed.

"Who are you? I don't recognize my wife and friend anymore," Christian argued.

Teagan looked at him through the mirror for a few seconds before placing the brush and paste back on the counter. She turned around and wrapped her arms around his neck.

"I promise to do better. This family is more important than anything else," Teagan pleaded.

Christian grasped her around the waist, pressing a kiss to her lips.

"I love you, Teagan."

"I love you more."

EIGHT

Closing the door of his Honda, Joshua fixed his work shirt, rubbing down the wrinkles. He followed two employees of the bank who held the door open for him. Trying to flirt, he slightly pinched her on the side of her waist.

"Not here, Joshua." Amy shook her finger at him.

"No one knows," Joshua said, going to the bank manager's office to work on a virus that corrupted his data. At twenty-four, Joshua was no taller than five-eight, slim, with a small belly, and well-trimmed blond hair. He wasn't the best-looking man, but he could get a girl to go out with him on a date, but never anything long term. He knocked on the door of Dave Grace, the branch manager, who waved him to enter. Joshua stood off to the side as Dave continued on the phone.

"I have the tech guy here now," Dave said, tapping a pen on the desk. Joshua scanned the room, remembering this was the second time he'd had to fix the branch manager's computer. Separate from the other employees, he predicted he was watching too much porn, and it finally died out on him.

"Let me call you back. Okay.... yeah." Dave hung up, walked around the desk, and extended a hand to Joshua.

"Sorry for making another trip out," Dave said.

"No problem. They pay me anyway," Joshua joked, placing his equipment on top of the desk.

"Well, I'll let you work. If you need anything, just call for me," Dave told Joshua, leaving his office.

Shutting the door, Joshua waited a few moments to see if anyone would walk back into the room. Checking his watch, he turned to sit down at the desk and plugged in his device monitor to see what was happening. Figuring out a reset would help, he hurriedly set in the information to the computer to mirror his own. While he waited, Joshua went through all the drawers and cabinets, checking one more time through the office window to see Dave talking with another employee across the room. The screen popped back on, Joshua typed in a code, and files popped up of accounts and addresses of customers. Whistling to himself on a good job, he copied as much information as he could and removed the device right when Dave came back to check on everything.

"Is she still working?" Dave questioned.

"All set, sir." Joshua rose, grabbing his equipment, passing a form for Dave to sign off that he completed the work.

PLACING the meat lover's pizza down on the table, Joshua locked his door, walking into the kitchen of the one-bedroom apartment. Grabbing a beer from the fridge, Joshua let the music blast in his ear from his favorite band. Joshua felt good about himself at scoring a big-time money-making job. He wasn't worried about getting caught or hearing how his parents disowned him since he refused to live the way they wanted him to live. The only person he kept up with was his sister because Abby refused to be ignored whenever she came to visit. At thirty-two, Abby was older than Joshua by a few years. Growing up, their parents always instilled college and having a family which was the path she went down. Joshua was extremely intelligent and charming but lacked in social skills.

Working as a computer specialist at Tech Hines, the company had accounts with all the major businesses in the city. Being freelance was the perfect role in his eyes because he loved having enough time to hack into computers around the world and play video games, which could bring in vast amounts of money. Abby tried calling him a few times, but he never answered. He said to himself that he'd call her back later in the week. She loved being a mom; leaving the workforce and staying home was the ideal life for her since Courtland worked as a pharmacy sales representative and traveled most days.

By accident one day, she watched the news, and a picture of Maksim Petrov strolled across. She remembered going to visit Joshua at his condo and seeing a group of men walking out toward a limo. At that moment, she had no other choice but to call anonymously to try to save her brother's life. Abby didn't want him mixed up in something that would hurt her family's name.

Joshua finished off another slice of pizza, wiping his hands on his shirt. Scattered on the floor in front of him were blueprints and information for Yankee Stadium. Maksim connected with him after seeing he was losing money gambling at Malcolm's casinos. Hearing him brag on how he was efficient in building things and computer hacking, Maksim had his men keep an eye on him for a few days before setting up a meeting and letting him know his debt was paid off. Now, Joshua and Duncan were under Maksim's hold, and he'd never let go unless it was through death.

Knock

Knock

Knock

Joshua lifted his head and checked the time on his watch. Rising up, he strolled to the door and looked through the peephole.

"Right on time," he muttered to himself, unlocking the door and pulling it open to Maksim, Saveli, and Nail. All three men, along with bodyguards, treaded into the living room. Joshua shut his door quickly, rushing to pick up his leftover clothes from last night and tossing them into his closet, reminding himself to get laundry done.

"Have a seat," Joshua said.

"I'll stand," Maksim spoke.

"Sure... uhm... okay."

"You have what we need?" Saveli questioned.

Nail stood, texting on his phone.

"Yeah, it's in my bedroom. Give me a second." Joshua walked down the hallway toward his bedroom. Not waiting for him to come back, Maksim nodded for his men to follow him. Everything was riding on his plans following through. After the American agent almost captured him and destroyed his plans, he needed to regroup and get out of the country for a little while. His cousin Nail and Saveli stayed here and kept him updated on what the police and FBI were working on since Duncan tapped into his connections. Finally, after a year of building a team, he set roots down in New York as the biggest gun and drug ring in the city.

"I have the layout and blueprints in the side pocket." Joshua motioned at the bag as he passed it over. Nail took it from his hands.

"Pay him, Saveli," Maksim said, walking out of the condo. Saveli nodded, reaching in his pocket for his phone, and logged into his text thread for their accountant.

"When are you planning this?" he called to their backs.

Maksim looked over his shoulder as he held the front door.

"I'd advise you to stay away now. I wouldn't want you to go up in smoke," Maksim sarcastically replied.

A chill ran up his arm, and a lump caught in his throat as he nodded back at Maksim, knowing he couldn't take back what he'd done. He needed to warn his sister just in case. Heading toward the window on the fourth floor, he watched as they piled into their cars. Maksim paused for a moment, glanced up toward the window, and smirked.

NINE

"Welcome to GNS, Seeking Truth with Sandra. I'm Sandra Gregg."

Sandra smiled as the director yelled cut, and she waited for makeup and hair. Tonight, she was presenting her evidence and trying to push her career to the next level; this was her moment to shine.

"We have two minutes," Winston, her co-host, told her.

With the music starting again, the red light came on as the countdown began. Sandra continued checking her makeup and clothes on the screen.

"Welcome to Seeking Truth with Sandra," she said.

"Sandra, we wanted to extend a congrats on your new show," Winston said.

"Thank you, Winston."

"What can viewers expect?"

"Glad you asked. Today, I wanted to show what our government is doing."

"The station has received a ton of comments."

"I have footage that you can see behind me of Congressman Duncan Brooks."

"Explain where you took this?" Winston asked.

"This was around nine or ten at a warehouse. Duncan was coming out alone."

"Did he explain what he was doing out there?"

"No, but I have a feeling it has something to do with Malcolm Holmes."

"The notorious drug dealer?" Winston's eyes rose in shock.

She nodded, crossing her hands in her lap.

"More details will be released soon, but I wanted the public to know where our tax money is going."

"Stay tuned for more Seeking Truth with Sandra Gregg."

The director yelled cut, and Sandra strolled to her office, removing her jacket and wiping the sweat off her nose. A knock came at her door.

"Good job on your first episode." Winston stood at the door with his hands in his pockets.

"Don't act like you care."

Sandra picked up her bottled water, taking a sip. With a twist to his lip, he stepped in closer, shutting her door. The two of them were rivals, always had been, and Sandra was underhanded with trying to make it to the top. Winston hated her but had a small crush deep down that he couldn't break.

"Where did you get the footage?"

"None of your business."

"Tell the truth, who'd you sleep with?"

"Get out of my office."

Winston leaned over on her desk with his hands planted on top.

"I bet you slept with Malcolm Holmes to get this footage."

"That's a lie!" Sandra spat.

He shrugged his shoulders.

"You get your story your way, and I make up mine."

"You're sick."

"And you're a bitch."

"There's that jealousy. Mad to see someone younger and beautiful moving up in the business," Sandra relayed.

"Don't flatter yourself." Winston turned to leave.

"Winston," Sandra called to his back.

He turned around.

"If I were you, I'd play my cards right and try to get along with me. Besides, GNS may not be here much longer." Sandra smiled with her hands on her hips.

DUNCAN THREW a glass across the room, and it shattered on the ground.

"That bitch!" he screamed, his assistant running in to see if he was hurt.

"Sir, is everything all right?" Camilla looked at Duncan disheveled and noticed glass on the ground.

"Leave me alone."

"But sir..."

"Get out!" Duncan shouted. Camilla rushed back out, shutting the door.

Pacing back and forth, he replayed the video from GNS again, seeing a screen grab of him leaving the building. He still hadn't been able to talk with his wife since they were going through a separation.

"I need to talk to Maksim," Duncan mumbled to himself. Running around to his desk, he picked up his cell and dialed Maksim's number.

"Mr. Congressman," he answered on the first call.

"We might have a problem."

"We or you?"

"I'm not playing around; someone saw me leaving the warehouse."

"So."

"That could be a problem for us."

"Not to me."

"If I go down..."

"Do you think it's wise to threaten me, Mr. Congressman?"

He lifted his head, shaking the water from his eyes, and the very volume of the lustral flood contented him.

"Don't call me anymore," Maksim stated, hanging up the phone.

"Wait!" Duncan pulled the phone away from his ear in disbelief.

Things were spiraling out of control, and he had no one to turn to. He decided to contact his ex for help.

"Please pick up," Duncan mumbled to himself. After three rings, the annoying voice he despised so much came through the line.

"What do you want, Duncan?" Cheryl demanded.

"Where are you?" he questioned.

"None of your business."

"Cheryl, this isn't the time to be combative."

"I'm going to hang up if you're going to have that tone with me."

"Okay... okay... sorry. I really need your help."

He was still tense and agitated; the paranoia within his mind did nothing to calm him down. Staring outside the office window, he felt like someone was watching and waiting to kill him.

"Call your parents. Better yet, the police."

"That's who I need help from."

"What are you talking about?" Cheryl pressed on.

Drifting over to the bar in the corner of his office, Duncan removed the top off the scotch bottle and took a whiff of the dark, strong, robust flavor.

"Has anything seemed off like somebody watching you?" Duncan investigated. Cheryl chuckled over the phone.

"I knew at some point your greedy ways would come back to hurt our family."

"Cheryl, I didn't do anything wrong. People I trusted betrayed me."

"Our divorce will be final soon—lose my number," Cheryl blurted out, ending the call.

"Cheryl! Cheryl! Fucking bitch!" Duncan groaned, tossing the drink back. Treading over to his desk, he pulled his key out and unlocked his secret compartment, pulling out a small bottle of cocaine.

"She'll regret this," Duncan mumbled to himself, dropping a little on the side of his wrist. With a rolled-up piece of paper, he dipped his head low and sniffed the contents up his nose. Leaning back in his chair with his eyes closed, he smiled.

THE SUN WAS SETTING as Teagan looked up the street. It was going on six in the afternoon, and she wanted to make it home in time to cook dinner and be with the kids before bedtime. Watching Sandra Gregg finish her conversation with a security guard out front of the GNS offices, she waited before stepping out and confronting her. Daughtrey stayed in the driver's seat, taking pictures and monitoring if anyone else was outside of the building after the video aired of Duncan Brooks. The president was pissed about the team not having a head's up and letting something like this get out to the public.

"Go time," Daughtrey said.

Pushing the door open and jogging across the street, Teagan called out her name while she strolled to her car.

"Sandra!"

Sandra peered over her shoulder.

"Agent Stone, what brings you down here?" Sandra stayed put with her grip on her keys.

"You want to tell me about the footage you have of Duncan Brooks?"

"No, I don't." Sandra started to turn and walk off.

"Sandra, you may think you're doing something to bring down bad people. But you're not."

"I know what I'm doing." Her eyes fell low, and Teagan could tell she wasn't so confident in her statement.

"You don't believe that."

"You're the last person to try to tell me how to do my job." Sandra approached, pointing her finger in her face.

"I want the footage, and I'm coming to you personally."

"Can't help you."

"I can go to your boss and get it with one phone call."

"Are you working with Duncan? Is that what this is about?" Sandra chuckled to herself.

"I'm focused on getting the truth."

"So, you're a truth teller now." Sandra sucked her teeth.

Teagan smiled coyly.

"Either you can give me the footage before the night is over, or I make one phone call and that dream job at the major network can go bye-bye," Teagan remarked, leaving Sandra speechless, watching Teagan jog back to her car.

———————

TURNING the spaghetti sauce on low, Teagan lifted the wooden spoon, enjoying the aroma of her family recipe.

"Almost ready," she said.

Tatum sat at the kitchen table coloring in her book. CJ and Cole were in the living room playing a video game. Everything was perfect in her eyes, and she looked forward to these types of days with no drama. The upcoming base-ball game was something she was looking forward to, and the boys kept talking about the seats and being up close to win an actual fly ball.

"Mommy, when's dinner going to be ready?" Tatum asked.

"Soon, baby."

"What did you cook?"

Tatum put her red crayon down and came to the stove next to her mother. Teagan ran a hand over her curly hair that she'd just washed the other day and let hang for the night.

"Spaghetti, vegan patties, and for dessert, sponge cake."

Tatum clapped her hands in excitement.

"Can I set the table?"

"Sure, baby." Tatum opened the side drawer of utensils and let Tatum count out what she needed.

"Five forks, right?" Tatum asked.

"Yes, you got it right."

"Boys, dinner is almost ready," Tatum yelled from the kitchen, and Teagan chortled under her breath.

"What's going on here?" Christian stood at the archway

of the kitchen, wearing jeans and a t-shirt after coming in from work.

"Dinner is almost ready, Daddy."

"Did you help Mommy with dinner, precious?" Christian strolled in further, kissing Teagan on the lips, wrapping his arms around her waist from the back.

"Yep," Tatum replied.

"Good girl," Christian said.

"How was your day?" Teagan turned in his arms, placing her hands around his neck.

"Long and boring. I did more hiring to take some of the load off me," he said.

"I'm very proud of you."

"Are you two going to kiss?" Tatum said.

"Maybe," Christian teased, releasing Teagan and tickling Tatum, lifting her in his arms as she laughed.

"Okay, Daddy, you win," Tatum laughed.

"Tatum, go wash up, and I'll set the plates," Teagan told Christian to release her as she ran out of the kitchen.

"Are you ready for the game with the kids?" Christian asked.

Mixing the noodles with the sauce, Teagan plated a large bowl and brought it to the table.

"Yeah, finally a real day off with the family."

"Good, I'm excited for the kids to be normal for once."

CJ and Cole ran in the kitchen, taking a seat at the table.

"Did you two wash your hands?" Teagan questioned, laying her apron down on the back of her seat.

"Yes, ma'am," both of them answered at the same time.

"All right, boys. Calm down and let's eat. Your mom made a lot of food."

"I sure did," she laughed, as Cole reached over to pick up the utensils in the spaghetti to feed himself.

"Cole, you're making a mess," Teagan fussed.

"A good mess though, right?" Cole jested.

"That's your son," Teagan said, and they all laughed as Tatum came back in the room and sat next to her mother. They talked about each other's day and what they would eat at the upcoming baseball game. Later on that night, everyone sank into Teagan and Christian's bedroom to watch a movie together as a family until they fell asleep.

TEN

Two days later.

Hazelnut-scented steamed latte filled the room as Teagan sipped, scanning through the video footage she was able to obtain from GNS. President Sanders pulled some strings and got the owner to release what they aired and to agree to not show any more video pertaining to Duncan Brooks or anything dealing with national security. Sandra was pissed when Teagan showed up with a lawyer from The Firm working on the behalf of DOJ. Informing her that this was a national security risk, the owner wanted nothing to do with the story any longer. Teagan felt like things were moving in a better direction, and knowing Duncan was starting to break gave her great pleasure.

"What are your thoughts?" Broderick asked, standing over her shoulder.

"It's him; the video is a little blurry, but you see a clear side view."

Broderick huffed out a breath.

"Malcolm's been a lot more forthcoming."

"He has no choice."

"What's the plan for Maksim?"

"Let's look at it from all angles." Teagan lifted the notepad and pen from her desk, drawing lines down the middle to describe her thoughts.

"We have Maksim, Duncan, and Joshua working together."

"Yeah, that we know of. Could be more people."

"No, I doubt that. Maksim's background fits the type to want to be in control."

Teagan stood, leaving the notepad on the desk. Broderick picked it up.

"He's out to do harm, and we know Duncan is in on it somehow."

"But to what extent?"

"Exactly. He's losing his reputation in the public, and his wife is divorcing him."

Broderick took notes, bobbing his head. Grabbing the other stack of files on Tech Hines Computer Services, Teagan pulled Joshua's information out, reading through the length of time he'd worked for the company.

"Joshua Kline has a sister named Abby."

"What did you find out about her?"

"She's married to a pharmaceutical sales rep, stay-at-home mom, typical housewife."

"What are you thinking? I can see it in your eyes."

Turning the file over for Broderick to see, she noticed Abby's phone records that went to her office.

"Interesting. This was the same date you received that anonymous call."

"What do you bet she was the one warning us about her brother?"

"Why would she rat her brother out?"

"Maybe trying to save him. She's older than him, and their parents seemed to cut him off."

Teagan folded her arms, staring at Broderick.

"You're thinking about paying her a visit."

"I thought about it, but that would only cause him to run. I want Maksim."

"We can put a tail on her."

"Just keep your distance," Teagan told him as he stood, gathering the information on Joshua's sister and leaving her office. Sitting back at her desk, she studied over Joshua's file, along with Duncan. Tech Hines had been around for twenty years, and Joshua started working there a few years ago. With a few complaints for being late, overall, he'd been the best computer specialist they had at the company. Grabbing her phone, she made a call over to Gregory's office.

"Broderick already told me to set up a tracker for Abby Kline," Gregory rushed out.

"Thanks, but I want you to look into Tech Hines Inc."

"Anything specific you want to look at?"

Teagan sighed and pursed her lip.

"No, I just want to make sure the company doesn't have anything to do with what Joshua is involved with."

"I can do that... Oh, I heard you got tickets for the opening game."

She smiled, dropping the papers on her desk.

"Yep, and I'm ready to take a few days off to be with my family."

"Those tickets were hard to come by. Make sure you get an autograph for me." Teagan chuckled at his comment.

"I promise to do my best but dealing with three kids in a crowded stadium is a challenge."

"That's true. Maybe I'll see if they have any last-minute tickets."

"Probably online you can see."

Logging into her email, her cell phone rang.

"Gregory, let me call you back. Christian is calling me."

"Copy that, boss. I'll email you any updates," Gregory teased, hanging up the phone.

"Hey, honey."

"I was thinking," Christian said.

"Okay ..." Teagan dragged out.

"I would like to take my wife out for lunch."

"Oh, we haven't gone on an afternoon date in a while. What's the occasion?"

"Just wanted to enjoy a little afternoon time together. You've shown me that you're cutting work down a little more."

"Yes, being the boss and delegating are my best skill sets," Teagan joked.

"Come meet me at Alamaza and show off those skills in person." Christian smiled through the phone, feeling the love of his words. She never wanted to argue or have Christian angry with her like he was a few weeks ago. It broke her to see the man she loved not have confidence in her commitment to their family. Sending a kiss through the phone, she hung up and sent an email to her team to inform them that she was leaving for lunch and to call on her cell phone if they needed her for anything.

Locking her office door, she went to the garage to have Sean drop her off at Alamaza, a local Mediterranean restaurant they'd frequented in the past.

TWENTY MINUTES LATER, Sean arrived in front of Alamaza, and Teagan jumped out, telling Sean she'd call when she was ready for him to pick her up. Treading into Alamaza, she thanked the security guard for holding the door open for her and scanned the room for Christian. Seeing him in the corner near the window, she motioned to the hostess that her party was already here and seated.

"I didn't see you leave this morning." Christian tugged on her leather jacket.

"Is that a good thing or a bad thing?" Teagan hugged Christian, pecking his lips and wiping the red lipstick away.

"Good thing, babe. It would make me want to skip out on work."

Teagan gasped, fluttering her eyes.

"My husband wants to play hooky? Who is this man and where is my Christian?"

"Ha... Ha... Funny, Teagan. We both used to be spontaneous."

"That's true, before the kids came along."

"Things were simpler when it was just us."

Taking the menu in her hands, she wanted to avoid going backwards and discussing her decision to become director and take on more responsibility.

"Have you ordered yet?" she asked.

"The drinks. I got your sweet tea and a beer for me."

They scanned over the menu as their waitress approached with their drinks.

"Hello, I'm Carol, your waitress this afternoon."

"Hi, we're ready to order."

"Awesome. What would you like to start with?"

Teagan ran her finger down the menu across the lunch specials.

"Let me have the seabass and pasta," Teagan said, closing the menu and passing it to Carol. Out of the corner of her eye, she noticed a familiar face.

"I'll get the same thing and some bread please," Christian ordered, giving Carol the menu, who turned and went back to the kitchen. Teagan slowly rose out of her seat as she saw Joshua Kline leave the bank across the street. Picking up her purse, she took out her phone and snapped a picture.

"What's wrong?" Christian asked, reaching for her hand.

"Uhm… give me one second, honey."

"Where are you going?"

Teagan sprinted out of the restaurant, leaving her purse with Christian yelling out her name. She hid behind a loading truck, staring at Joshua talking on the phone. He seemed upset, with a scowl on his face.

"Talk to me," she muttered to herself.

Checking the time on her watch, she sent a text to Gregory with the photos of Joshua to see what job he had to do at the bank today. Soon as she closed out of the text thread, a car pulled up with a woman stepping out, marching over to him and yelling in his face. Wanting to get a better look, she eased down to the other end of the truck as the worker removed the loading cart.

"Sorry," Teagan said, bumping into the driver.

Her eyes rose in shock, seeing Abby Kline meeting her brother.

"I need to hear what they're saying."

Right as she started to get closer, a hand gripped her arm, turning her around.

"What the hell are you doing?" Christian fussed.

Teagan looked over her shoulder, hoping Joshua didn't see her.

"Christian, this is an emergency. Go back inside."

"I thought this was us spending time together?"

She kept glancing over, and Joshua finally noticed and

made eye contact with her. His face drained in acknowledg-
ment of who she was.

"Shit!" she barked.

Joshua ran and jumped into his car, leaving his sister
standing there. Teagan waited for the cars to pass by, when
Joshua pulled off fast, almost knocking her over. Christian
grabbed her back by the waist, falling down on the ground.

"Who was that?"

He helped her up off the ground, running his hands
across her chin, arms, and back.

"A case I'm working on." Teagan bent down to pick up
her phone from the ground, noticing the screen cracked a
little.

"You hurt anywhere? Do you need to go to the
hospital?"

Teagan shook her head no.

"I'll be fine. I need to get back to the office," she
answered, limping slightly back to the curb of the street.

"Let me drop you off then."

"I'll call Sean."

"Teagan, get in the car. You're the one who ran out
without saying anything."

Staring at each other for a few seconds, Teagan ran a
hand over her face, nodding her head, walked around to the
other side of his Range Rover and slid in when he unlocked
the door.

***

SHE SCANNED the faces of her team as they all sat in the
conference room with a projector, showing the photos of
Joshua Kline outside talking with his sister. Once Christian
left from dropping her off, she promised to check with the

on-staff medic if she felt any pain from earlier today. Rubbing the back of her neck, she popped two Advils to control the building migraine.

"He only worked on one computer today," Gregory stated.

"Anything suspicious left on his computer?" Spider asked.

Gregory typed on the computer, reloading documents of accounts.

"He's good, but I was able to see that he copied some high-profile accounts."

"Did the bank manager get in contact with the owners?" Teagan questioned, rubbing her temples.

"I told him to close those accounts just in case," Gregory answered.

"What do you want to do?" Spider turned toward Teagan.

"Time to end this," Teagan replied.

Everyone in the room agreed, and Teagan leaned forward with her hands crossed.

"Gregory, I want you to lock him out of everything. Spider, get whatever warrants we need."

"Should we go after his sister?" Spider wondered.

"No, that will just tip him off. Daughtrey, get the logistics together."

"And Broderick?" Spider said.

"Let him know it's time to put in his notice with Malcolm," Teagan responded and stared around the room, focusing on each man she'd worked alongside. Going into another death situation never got old, but Teagan knew they had each other's back. The only way to survive was to not let death scare you.

ELEVEN

The day of the opening game finally arrived as Maksim stood amongst his men in a circle inside the warehouse. They'd been previously discussing how this large-scale job would either bring them beyond riches or complete destruction. Either way, Maksim Petrov would make a mark on the country to the world if everything stuck to the plan. The device that Joshua created sat in a bag in front of Saveli. He was in charge of making sure it was placed in the right position before detonating at the precise moment all the lights went out.

"Nail, you with me, driving toward the east side," Maksim explained.

"How many men do you have with Saveli?" Nail asked.

"Two, dressed normally. Remember we have it timed correctly at one."

"Should we take care of any leftover issues?" Saveli asked, cocking his gun back.

Maksim smirked, knowing Saveli was ready to end Duncan and Joshua's lives.

"There will be time for that later."

"I never liked that congressman," Saveli spoke, waving his hand in front of his face like Duncan smelled bad. Everyone laughed, including Maksim.

"He won't be a problem from what I've seen."

"That reporter lady," Nail brought up.

"She can be spared," Maksim said.

"What if we take her with us?" Nail made kissing sounds.

"First, we get our money, and then you do whatever you want."

"Everybody has uniforms, correct?" Maksim queried, showing photos of security uniforms on screen of the bank they'd planned to rob.

"I'd rather wear my own clothes," Nail replied, scoffing.

"Only for a little while, cousin," Maksim stated.

"Any updates from Malcolm Holmes?" Saveli brought up.

"We can let him live for now."

"To Petrov!" Nail held up his glass of rum in front of him for a toast.

All the men picked up their glasses in support of their boss and leader.

"To Petrov!" everyone yelled, finishing their drinks.

"Load up the trucks," Maksim called out, while scanning over the blueprints of the bank and the baseball stadium.

"What are you thinking?" Saveli approached, standing beside him.

"They'll never know it was us; it's perfect."

"And the spy bitch?"

Maksim waved off his comment.

"She's too stuck on other things. By the time we get the

bomb set ..." Maksim made an exploding bomb motion with his mouth and hand.

"The private jet is ready, and the boat has escape routes."

"Just remember, not everyone will be leaving with us."

"I understand, boss. Kill all witnesses," Saveli said, shaking hands with Maksim and stalking out of the warehouse.

WHILE MAKSIM DIRECTED his team on the next steps, Malcolm stood outside of Bambi's house holding flowers to make up for never calling again after another night of passion. Dealing with government officials and foreign mobsters had him stressed and looking over his shoulder every five minutes. When Teagan confronted him in her office, he thought that led to him being charged with a crime. Now giving over as much evidence of Maksim's whereabouts, he could try to make up with Tonya since she ignored his calls.

"Tonya, I know you're in there," Malcolm said, standing outside her apartment. She lived in a semi-decent area. It wasn't the worst but not the easiest place when you're well established like him. After a few people had been robbed or killed, trying to convince her to move was out of the question, but she refused any handouts.

"Go away, Malcolm," Tonya said on the other side of the door.

"Baby, I'm sorry," Malcolm pleaded.

"I don't care."

"Listen... I have tickets to the opening game today."

She loved baseball growing up, and Malcolm used that

to his advantage when he bribed a friend who scalped his tickets.

"What row?" she asked.

"Upper deck."

"Let me see; hold them up to the door."

"Tonya."

"Malcolm, you want to come in and apologize, so start with the tickets."

Malcolm held the flowers between his arms and dug in his pockets for the tickets. Holding them up to the peephole, he heard the locks turning.

"These are for you," Malcolm said.

"Ummm... Mmhm." Tonya took the flowers out of his hands.

"I apologize for going missing on you."

"Malcolm, what are we doing?"

"What do you mean?"

"Either we're going to be together or not."

"We are together."

Malcolm strolled over to Tonya, lifting her left hand, and placed a kiss on the back of her palm.

"So, we spent an amazing night together, and I never heard from you."

"Because of business."

Tonya snatched the tickets away from him.

"Get out."

"Damnit, Tonya!"

"I'm the only one who can yell in this house."

He backed up, holding his hands up in surrender.

"Sorry, let's go to the game and enjoy a nice day out."

"Game, then you're treating me to a nice dinner at the most expensive place."

"Whatever makes you happy."

"Yeah…"

Tonya went to grab her purse and jacket from the couch. Malcolm pulled her back into his arms, holding her chin in place, pressing a long, lingering kiss.

"I'm really sorry."

"I forgive you," Tonya responded with a curl of upper lip.

Holding hands, they walked out of her apartment and down to his Mercedes Benz. Helping her inside, some of his men stood around in front of their cars.

"I thought we were going to the game," Tonya questioned, staring at Ishmael and Broderick talking to another man.

"We are."

"So, why are your men here? Are you in trouble?"

Malcolm started his car, putting his seatbelt on and adjusting his mirror.

"Baby, you know I have to be cautious at all times."

"Is there something I should know about, Malcolm?" Tonya inquired, locking her seatbelt across her waist.

"Enjoy the day, baby. I plan on spoiling you," Malcolm remarked, turning on his right signal and making a U-turn in the street. Watching out of his window, he saw everybody following him through the streets. He felt a little relief with the extra protection. Placing his hand on Tonya's thigh, he rubbed up and down.

"Thanks for the tickets," Tonya said.

"Anything for you, sweetheart," Malcolm answered.

ACROSS TOWN, Sandra Gregg was already at the big opening game, getting her makeup touched up. The owner didn't want her in the studio for a few days, so the program manager assigned her mundane news stories to keep her out of the way. Today's opening baseball game would keep her busy for hours since a ceremony pitch from the New York governor was planned, along with a retirement ceremony. She hated things that dealt with soft reactions from the public. No way she would make it as a bigtime journalist covering a game that was played every year with the same drug-addicted, steroid-induced, airhead players. Teagan Stone stuck to her word and got the footage pulled, but she had plans to go even deeper into The Firm and Congressman Brooks once she finished this story.

"All right, Sandra, are you ready to do a run through?" the camera guy asked. Sandra stood from the makeup chair, taking the microphone from his hands.

"How does this angel look?" Sandra questioned, posing in front of the baseball sign of New York Sparks.

"A little to the left," Mike answered.

She shuffled to the left.

"How about now?" she questioned, fluffing her hair out.

"Great, it's just a few run throughs for now." Counting down from three, two, one.

"I'm Sandra Gregg, and today we're here at the Sparks opening game." Sandra waved her hand up at the stadium sign.

"Good, but a little cheerier."

Sandra rolled her eyes.

"Here today from GNS, I'm Sandra Gregg at the Sparks opening game."

"Much better."

"Perfect, let me grab a bottle of water for a second. It's hot," Sandra complained even though she wore a pants suit like she was meeting the president of the United States.

"Take five," Mike said.

Switching to the van, she opened the cooler and took out a bottle of water. Watching the crowd of people lined up at the front line, she spotted the last person she intended to see.

What is she doing here?

Holding her hand over her eyes to block out the sun, she watched as Teagan rubbed the top of a little girl's head. A man and two boys stood next to them.

"Are you ready to film?" Mike said.

"Give me a second," Sandra stated, leaving her water and the microphone in the van, stalking over to Teagan and her family.

"Excuse me, sorry, excuse," Sandra said to some people in line.

"Watch it, lady," a young boy yelled out with his friends when she pushed him to the side.

"You bitch!" Sandra shouted; the crowd gasped in shock.

Teagan turned her head in the direction of the statement. Seeing the news reporter she'd been arguing with calling her out in public wasn't on her plans for the day.

"Excuse me," Teagan said.

"You tried to ruin my career." Sandra pointed in Teagan's face. Christian tried to block Sandra from his kids, pulling Tatum to the left side of him as the line moved toward the entrance.

"I have no idea what you're talking about, but I'm here with my children."

"You know exactly what you did. How about I tell everyone here who you really are?" Sandra taunted, tapping her foot, with hands on her hips.

"Sandra! Sandra!" Mike shouted her name.

She waved him off.

"We have a show to do." Mike pointed to the camera.

Sandra groaned, nostrils flaring, and peered at Teagan.

"This isn't over," Sandra promised.

"I look forward to the next round," Teagan teased, hearing Christian call her name when the window booth opened for them to submit their tickets.

Sandra stomped off back to the GNS news van, picking up the microphone and moving the earpiece into her ear, preparing to do another announcement.

"Ready?" Mike said.

"Just roll the camera," Sandra hissed.

Mike motioned his hands, counting down.

"Welcome to GNS News with opening day for the New York Sparks!" Sandra grinned wide, pointing at the stadium.

"We have families of all ages, ready for the opening pitch. I hope you stay tuned."

"Cut. Now let's get some footage from inside," Mike said, shifting the camera lower to hold.

For over an hour, they filmed different angles of the entrance, interviewed a few fans, and met with a few members of the management.

"When is this thing going to start?" Sandra blew out a frustrated breath, annoyed at the long wait time.

"Baseball goes for over two hours sometimes. Didn't you know this?"

"I have better things to do," Sandra spat.

"I'm going to the restroom. Watch the equipment," Mike said, leaving her alone to fuss.

While standing in the corner facing the entrance, she noticed Malcolm Holmes holding hands with a woman wearing a shirt with the Sparks logo.

"A drug dealer at a baseball game. Maybe this day can get better after all," Sandra said, looking at Malcolm in line to order some food.

"Hurry up, Mike," she mumbled to herself.

Five minutes later, Malcolm and Tonya went inside to take their seats, leaving Sandra even more pissed that she missed an opportunity to spy on him. Mike, still inside the bathroom, hadn't come out, and Sandra stomped over to the bathroom when she bumped into a guy by accident.

"Ouch! What were you going to do?" Sandra barked. Glancing up, she noticed it was the same young man who flipped her off in the car a few days ago.

"Cyka." Nail replied bitch in Russian.

TWELVE

An hour earlier.

Teagan helped Tatum fix her hair while the boys went outside to get in the car. Teagan told the team to contact her if there was an emergency, but otherwise, she'd be off the radar to spend time with her family at the game. Christian was still a little extra sensitive from the situation at the restaurant. Coming home early last night and ordering food while the kids stayed with his parents helped loosen him up a little. He was back to being his old self, but she made sure to not push his buttons. Checking out her appearance in the mirror, she tightened her ponytail and touched up her makeup. Wearing a Sparks t-shirt like the family and blue jeans, she was ready to be a normal family without having to fight corruption.

"Mommy, let's go," Tatum said.

"Here I come. Did you get your purse?" Teagan queried, placing her new phone inside her black bag.

"Yes. See?" Tatum held up her little black purse that matched her mom's.

"Good job. Do you have your allowance for your snacks?"

"Yep, I saved up twenty dollars," Tatum insisted, opening her purse to show off.

"Ohh, good job, sweetie."

Tatum grabbed her mother's hand, leaving the living room together and locking the front door as Christian shut the trunk. Tatum skipped over to the car, and Christian held the back door open and helped her climb into her booster seat.

"Princess, you look beautiful."

"Thanks, Daddy."

Teagan opened the passenger door, and Christian came around to the front.

"We all set?" Christian asked the family, putting his shades on.

"Yes!" the kids answered at the same time.

"Here we go."

"The governor is throwing out the first pitch," Teagan said, turning on the radio.

"This is the biggest opening of the season, they say," he replied.

He pulled out of the driveway and turning left toward the side street. Christian ran a hand down Teagan's arm.

"Looking cute, baby," Christian remarked.

"Thank you."

"Ewe... please don't kiss," CJ said, covering his eyes with his hands.

"How do you think you three got here?" Christian joked, turning at the light to get on the freeway.

"Let's not torture the babies."

"Can we meet some of the players?" Cole asked.

"I doubt it, Cole. It's an opening game, and they're usually busy with long lines."

Tatum sang in the car, as Cole and CJ argued about changing the music as Teagan glanced at her phone, wondering if everything was going well with the team.

"Are they out on assignment?" Christian stopped at a red light.

"You know I can't talk about missions."

"I can see it in your eyes. You're here physically, but not mentally."

"Christian, don't start."

"I'm not starting, just making observations." The car went silent as Christian got off the freeway, turned left, and arrived at the Sparks stadium near the Bronx. They stepped out and opened the door toward the back to help the kids. They grabbed their hands to stick together. Teagan pulled the tickets out of her purse and handed them to Christian to let him take the lead.

"This line is long."

"We're still early, so we didn't miss anything," Christian said, pointing to the line.

"I'm hungry," Cole said.

"Once we get through the line, we can get food," Teagan replied.

"Here we go, section B," Christian said.

Teagan held onto Tatum's hand, standing next to Christian in the crowds as people screamed and yelled in excitement. The entire building was flooded with young kids, and Teagan admired how well-behaved her children were. Going out as a family was rare because the boys would end up in some type of argument. Then Tatum would throw a tantrum if she didn't get her way.

"You bitch!" Looking ahead, she didn't think anyone was calling out her name.

"Agent Stone."

Teagan stiffened in place being called Agent Stone in public.

"Excuse me," Teagan said.

"You tried to ruin my career." Sandra pointed in Teagan's face. Christian tried to block Sandra's hand and adjust the kids to the other side.

"I have no idea what you're talking about. I'm here with my children."

Growing more frustrated with Agent Stone's passive-aggressive attitude, Sandra closed the space between them.

"You know exactly what you did. How about I tell everyone here who you really are?" Sandra whispered for just Teagan to hear.

"I suggest you move along."

"Or what?"

"Sandra! Sandra!" a voice called from behind Sandra.

"You're lucky I have to work." Sandra tossed her hair over her shoulder, scowling at Teagan. Shaking her head, Teagan caught up with Christian and the kids walking in the direction of the opened ticket booth and getting their wristbands for entry.

"Can I get popcorn?" Cole said.

"Can I get a hotdog?" CJ asked.

"I want ice cream," Tatum called out.

"All right, you three. We aren't going crazy with junk food," Teagan pointed out.

"We still have to go out to dinner afterwards, so get something light," Christian backed her up.

"Okay," CJ answered.

"Babe you want to get the seats, and I'll get the food," Teagan suggested.

"Sure, be careful." Christian pecked her on the lips.

"Don't worry."

WHILE GRABBING the food for the kids, Teagan chuckled to herself at Sandra confronting her. At the same time, Nail wrapped the rope around Mike's neck in the bathroom as Saveli put the bomb in place down near the seats. Maksim was staying in contact and driving to the second location of the bank with Sergei and Vanya. Mike caught Nail putting a bomb in place underneath the counter in the bathroom, and Nail decided in a rush to kill him.

"Shush, no one is going to save you," Nail warned as Mike's legs stopped wiggling, and he pulled him into the bathroom stall. Shutting the door, he went back to setting the timer, throwing away the bookbag, and washing his hands. Coming out of the bathroom calmly, he put the out of order sign on the door and marched toward Saveli when he bumped shoulders with a woman.

"Ouch. Watch where you're going," she screamed.

Grunting, he stared into the face of the woman he knew from TV, the one Maksim had them keeping an eye on. Flipping her off during traffic, they thought she took to their threat, after posting the video of Duncan. Standing in front of her now, she was more aggravating than before.

"Cyka." Nail called her a bitch in Russian. Going in the opposite direction as her, he jogged a little faster to find Saveli.

Pushing through crowds, he ran down the stairs and caught up with Saveli coming his way.

"Hey, you left your bag!" a guy yelled out at Saveli.

"Shit!" Saveli whispered.

"Hey, man." The older guy looked like he was in his fifties. A bald head, not taller than five-eight, thin lips, and a beer belly. Heading down the steps holding the food one row over, Teagan heard the man call out to somebody and noticed Nail and Saveli walking away. Seeing those two faces as Maksim's men and the older guy trying to get their attention with a bag in his hand, caused her to drop the food.

"Sir! Don't move." Teagan held her hand out for him to stop, running over in his direction.

"Teagan, what are you doing?" Christian stood, hearing her voice.

More people walked in to find their seats.

"Christian, call the police!" Teagan yelled, making it to the older gentleman.

Christian removed his phone, knowing something was happening that wouldn't be good to have his kids involved.

"Sir, where did you get the bag?" Teagan questioned, taking her phone out of her pocket and dialing Spider's number.

"How's the game going?" Spider asked.

"Spider, we have a situation," Teagan said.

"I'm turning around now," Spider replied.

"Get everyone locked and loaded. Maksim is here."

"Shit! Are the kids safe?" Spider queried.

"They're with me. But I need all hands on deck."

"I just saw it sitting on the ground; the guy left it," Henry told Teagan.

A few security guards came over at the commotion.

"What's the problem, ma'am?" A guard wearing a red vest with the Sparks logo held his radio in his hand.

"I don't want to alarm you, but there's a bomb in this bag." Teagan hung up with Spider.

"What!" the older guy yelled and almost dropped the bag.

"Don't move! Just focus on me," Teagan said in a soothing voice.

"Hey, what are you doing?" A woman Teagan assumed was his wife came over to them.

"Margaret, go sit down. There's an emergency," Henry said.

"Ma'am, please take your seat," the security guard stated.

"The police are coming," Christian said.

"How do you know there's a bomb in the bag?" the security guard wondered.

"I work for Special Agency. The two men who walked away are a part of the biggest cartel family in the world."

"What do you need?"

"We need this place on lockdown."

"The governor is coming," the security guard remarked.

"Call and cancel, the less people the better." Teagan turned to face Christian.

"I know," Christian said.

"I promise I'll make it up to you." Teagan kissed him on the lips.

"I got the kids. You're safe," Christian demanded, holding the back of Teagan's neck and capturing her lips, tonguing her down before releasing her to go off. This could be the last time they were together, and he realized how proud he was of his wife and how she put herself on the line for others. Teagan wiped the lipstick off and grabbed another security guard to follow her as she gave direction.

"You come with me. We need to lock this down and find them." Teagan ran up the stairs.

"Teagan!" Christian called out, holding her purse.

She glanced over her shoulder and smiled, knowing he was telling her to not forget her gun. Heading back toward him, she took her purse from him, kissing each child on the cheek and telling them she loved them.

"I'll be back," Teagan said.

"Mommy, what's going on?" Tatum inquired.

"Nothing, baby. Mommy just has to work," Teagan explained, kissing Tatum once more before following the security guard.

"I want everyone in a single line checking IDs against these pictures," Teagan said.

"Can you send these pictures to my phone?" the security guard asked.

"What's your name?"

"Bobby."

"Bobby, what you're doing today isn't only for your country, but for the world."

"Yes, ma'am."

"Teagan! Teagan!" Spider yelled her name, running to her with Daughtrey and the rest of the boys.

"Catch us up," Spider said.

"We were looking on a small scale, but this son of bitch planted a bomb."

"You mean here?" Daughtrey questioned.

"Yeah." Teagan bent over, catching her breath.

"How did you find out?" Spider insisted, following in her direction.

"By accident, I spotted Nail and Saveli," she responded.

"Henry, the guy sitting over there, picked up the bag," Teagan replied.

A few people grumbled in line, wondering what was going on.

"We found something!" another security guard said.

Running in that direction, Teagan felt her cell phone vibrate.

"What do you get?" Teagan pushed through the crowd, stepping into the men's bathroom and finding Mike dead.

"As we were checking, the door was jammed, and we found his body," the guard spoke.

Unknown: Did you find my little present?

Teagan: Who is this?

Unknown: Come on now, Agent Stone. Let's not play dumb.

Teagan's brows drew into slits.

"Gregory, trace my phone," Teagan shouted.

"On it," Gregory said, running out of the bathroom.

"He's toying with us," Spider said.

"Something's not right. We need to find Joshua," Teagan muttered.

"What did you say?"

"Follow me, I want to speak with Joshua Kline."

Teagan pivoted, leaving the bathroom, and saw Sandra talking with a police officer as she walked by.

"This is all your fault," Sandra spat, throwing her hands in the air.

Jumping in the SUV, Daughtrey and Spider followed alongside, taking the lead as they left, going in the direction of Joshua's last-known address.

"Get every location for the material needed to create those bombs."

"Are they on a timer?"

"Yeah, we have maybe an hour."

"Buckle up," Daughtrey said, pushing the gas on the car, swerving through traffic.

"Make sure the airlines have photos of Petrov's family," Teagan explained.

"Calling now," Spider said.

"Did he text back?" Daughtrey mentioned.

"No."

"He can't get away with this. What was that reporter doing there?" Daughtrey wondered.

"Filming the opening season," Teagan sighed, releasing a long-held breath.

"Abby Kline hasn't heard from her brother," Spider said, making another call.

"I hate to make this next call."

"To whom?"

"The president," Teagan said somberly, looking out of the window.

THIRTEEN

Game Day.

Time was running out for Joshua Kline when he saw the breaking news about a bomb at New York Sparks Stadium. He knew that was his handiwork, and he needed to get out of the country. A few days ago, he'd almost been caught but rented a hotel room for a few nights before grabbing a few more items from his apartment. When the story came on the screen, that was his cue to take the little money he had from the sale to fly to a place that didn't have extradition. Stuffing two suitcases, he looked around his apartment for any last-minute details. Opening the door of his apartment, his eyes widened in shock.

"Going somewhere, Joshua?" Teagan questioned, pointing a gun in his face.

"Please don't kill me," Joshua answered, dropping the bags.

"That depends on how much you can tell me about those bombs."

Spider and Daughtrey searched through his place as Teagan continued talking with him.

"I don't know about anything."

Teagan shot him in the foot without even blinking.

"Ahhh! You shot me," Joshua screamed, falling on the ground, holding his foot.

"Joshua, focus... look up here," Teagan said, snapping her fingers in his face.

"I need to go to the hospital. Please, you can't do this," Joshua pleaded.

"The only place you're going is to jail. That little flesh wound will be found, but the next bullet won't."

"I got some blueprints," Spider said, coming from the back.

"Now tell me again you don't know anything."

"I needed the money."

"Did you think about your family at all?"

"He promised me some money, and all I needed to do was put a bomb together."

"A bomb that can kill over twenty-thousand people!" Teagan punched him in the face.

The door opened wide, and the police stepped in.

"Take him in and book him for terrorist activities," Teagan said, pointing at Joshua.

"Wait! I'll help you."

"Too late," Teagan responded, watching the police handcuff him and drag him out of the living room.

"Look at this; they're papers with Duncan's signature at Tech Hines," Spider said.

"I bet Duncan is somehow behind Tech Hines."

Reading over the paperwork, Teagan deciphered that Duncan came in as an investor a year ago, even though Joshua had worked at the company a few years prior.

"Duncan probably was looking for a quick pay day." Teagan pointed at the amount of shares Duncan owned.

"A twenty-percent share," Daughtrey whistled.

"Let's go have a chat with Duncan."

All three left while the forensic team continued tossing the place around for more evidence.

Running back to the car and jumping in, Teagan's phone vibrated again.

Unknown: Tell me, how is Joshua doing?

Teagan logged into her thread, seeing the unknown number.

Teagan: In jail, you'll join him soon.

Unknown: Tell my friend Duncan it was nice working with him.

Teagan: You're not getting away with this.

Unknown: I already have.

Teagan: We won't stop until you're caught.

Unknown: I'd hate for your husband to find you in pieces.

Teagan: Tell it to my face.

Unknown: Have a good day, Agent Red.

MAKSIM SAT in the armed truck wearing the fake uniform, chuckling at his text message thread. His men set up blockades along the street, while Saveli and Nail handled the baseball situation.

"America's pastime," Maksim chortled to himself.

He watched the news footage of what was going on at the stadium through social media on his phone. Maksim grinned at his plan coming together, and all the loose ends would soon be eliminated. Joshua got himself arrested, but it was nothing to have him killed in jail. No matter if Agent Stone found Duncan, anyone could be touched for the right price. Sending another text to Agent Stone was a dangerous game, but he didn't care. It was a game of cat and mouse, a challenge in his eyes ever since she came after him a few months back. Right now, he needed the men to pick up the pace before they suspected what was really going on. Checking the time, he had it synced with the traffic lights to go out as a backup plan. The flights would already have police swarming, so that was out of the question. As a backup, he had a boat paid for with a driver to take him to Miami, then Dominican Republic, and he'd fly out of the country. Maksim continued watching his men when his phone rang.

"Speak."

"We're swarmed with police," Saveli whispered.

"Where are you?"

"The place is surrounded, but we found a closet."

"You need to figure out a way to get out, or you know what to do."

Everyone made a sacrifice that instead of being caught, they'd go out by suicide. No one was to ever end up in prison. The Petrov family long-standing ritual was family first and loyalty.

"Yes, boss."

"Do what is necessary," Maksim said, ending the call.

"Maksim, we have ten more minutes before we can go," Sergei explained.

"Everybody ready?" he asked.

"Yes. How is Saveli doing?"

"Focus on your job. Saveli is handling himself," Maksim changed the subject.

Pulling out the gun from his waist, he cocked it back, making sure the safety was off. He looked at his watch.

"Soon, there will be a huge fireworks. Sergei, we've pulled it off," Maksim told him.

Sergei smiled, ready to go to the bank and take everything he'd always wanted. Maksim said there would be more than enough money that everyone could retire many times over with what was inside the bank.

"What about the Americans that helped you?

"Unfortunately, they're dead men walking."

FOURTEEN

Teagan slowly nudged the door open with her gun prepared. With no answer she went forward with Daughtrey and Spider behind her as they noticed Duncan's body laid on the ground with a bullet to the head. Her personal feelings aside, Teagan sighed, looking around the room. She strode closer to the body as Spider checked his pulse and shook his head.

Thinking of the amount of time they had left to find what bank was being robbed, as the bomb was being deactivated, her nerves were on high alert dealing with multiple crises at once and wanting to get her family to safety. Sauntering over to his desk, she pulled the drawers open and rummaged through filing cabinets for any evidence. Duncan was too stupid to not keep something around with his name on it. Her eyes narrowed at the locked bottom drawer. Yanking harder, it still didn't open. She looked around the desk, picked up the mail opener, and popped the lock. Inside was a thick blue envelope. She scanned it as Spider and Daughtrey called for a cleanup crew.

"What's that?" Spider pointed at the envelope.

Teagan shrugged, opening it up and seeing banking information for TransUnion on Fifth Avenue with checking account numbers highlighted. Teagan turned toward his computer and typed in the name of the bank, went to login, and it was already saved with his username. She tried to put in his last name as the password and received an error message.

"Shit!"

"What happened?" Spider stalked over to the desk.

"I need his password." Teagan tried looking in his files saved on his computer to get some sense of giveaway. With Joshua in custody and Duncan dead, only Maksim was left, and he was on the run while they locked down the airports.

The door opened for the cleanup team to arrive and take things over as they continued finding Duncan's secrets.

"We know he's money hungry, right?" Spider asked, standing with his hands crossed over his chest.

Teagan glanced up at him.

"Yeah."

"Then it wouldn't be his name or birthday. Duncan lived off being one step ahead through this entire time."

Teagan fell silent in thought of what could get them inside his account. Coming up empty, she pulled her cell out of her pocket and dialed Gregory to have him hack into the account instead.

"We're still working here, Teagan," Gregory blurted out.

"I need you to let them handle it and get to a computer."

"What's up?" Gregory yelled through the phone at someone to take over for him.

"Duncan is dead, and Maksim is gone. We're at his office trying to hack into a bank account," Teagan explained.

"Text me the information."

"TransUnion on Fifth Avenue; we're heading there now. See what you can find," Teagan requested, ending the call and dialing number one on her phone.

"Agent Red," President Sanders answered.

Teagan jumped up from the desk, grabbing the papers and heading out with Spider and Daughtrey behind.

"I need the TransUnion shut down and free rein," Teagan commanded without waiting for an answer.

"Anything else?" President Sanders replied.

"No, sir."

"And Maksim?" President Sanders asked.

"Still on the run. I have my people checking every spot."

They stepped on the elevator, heading to the lobby.

"Call me once you have an update." The president ended the call, and Teagan pressed the button for the lobby.

Five minutes later, as Teagan stepped off the elevator, the entire building was surrounded with local police, FBI, and DEA agents. Usually issues like this would be under lock with only the FBI handling the case, but with Maksim being connected, Teagan made it a priority to oversee. Marching out the doors, a strum of reporters pushed cameras and microphones in their faces. Teagan pushed through the crowd and reached for the driver's side door handle when a camera was forced in her face.

"Agent Red, is it true Duncan Brooks is dead?" Sandra smirked, holding the microphone toward Teagan.

Freezing at the question, Teagan stepped around the door, snatching the microphone from her hand.

"How do you know that?" Teagan's brow hiked in suspension.

"From a reliable source," Sandra said.

Teagan stared at Sandra, taking in her demeanor with her blond hair pulled back into a tight bun, red lipstick, and black suit.

"What color lipstick are you wearing?" Teagan questioned.

Sandra was surprised by the question, as the camera man shrugged his shoulders.

"Candy Cane Red by Ray Cosmetics. Why?" Sandra answered, shuffling from one foot to the next, her hand planted on her hip.

Teagan's mind raced back to Duncan at the training session. She closed her eyes, remembering his aggravated attitude and disheveled clothes with a red stain on his collar. Knowing it was from lipstick and the amount of knowledge Sandra possessed about everything, it was only right she fit the last piece of the puzzle. Teagan turned toward Daughtrey, motioning to grab Sandra and take her with them.

"Sandra, you're under arrest." Teagan went to open the door again.

"Wait a minute! You can't do this," Sandra screamed as flashes from the cameras and loud yelling rang out as Teagan slid in the passenger seat and dialed Gregory's number again.

"Almost got it, Teagan," Gregory called out.

"Try Sandra," Teagan responded.

She heard typing through the phone.

"How did you know that was the password?"

"Lucky guess."

As Daughtrey drove off into traffic, Teagan grabbed her seatbelt. Sandra was playing everybody, only out for herself. Fooling around with Duncan was just to get ahead, and once he cut her off for playing the video of him at the warehouse, she knew her luck of having access would dwindle.

"He has money in an offshore account, twenty million," Gregory said.

"Any trace to Maksim?"

"Bingo... Duncan received money from a Russian account. I'm willing to bet Maksim is behind the money," Gregory explained.

Speeding in traffic, Teagan kept an eye on the car behind them that held Sandra inside.

"We're almost there. Can you tell how much is in the bank right now?"

Daughtrey ran a red light as cars honked their horns. Taking a sharp right, he went down a back alley two blocks over and slowed down, scoping out the scene.

"Right there," Spider muttered from the backseat. Two bank trucks were parked in the back.

"The bank has between two hundred to five hundred million cash on hand," Gregory said. Daughtrey backed up and parked the car with the engine running, watching two men dressed in employee uniforms.

"Are the alarms off?" Teagan asked him.

"Yeah. Do you want me to trigger them and get SWAT down there for backup?" Gregory wondered.

"No. we can handle it but get me visual on the inside to my phone," Teagan demanded, ending the call. Two more black SUVs pulled up next to them, and Daughtrey pointed for them to park.

"What's the plan?" Daughtrey said.

Teagan sat in her seat and peered at the setups and the twenty-story bank building. Going in unprepared would get them all killed, but not finding Maksim could send things into a bigger tailspin.

"We're going in; get suited up."

Everyone stepped out of the car, and one of the drivers

in the other SUV parked sideways, cutting off traffic. He stepped out with orange cones, signaling the road was closed. Teagan grabbed the bulletproof vest from the back and took the rifle from Spider's hand.

"Sandra's still with us," Spider said.

"Duncan was sleeping with her and feeding her information."

"Damn," Daughtrey whistled in shock.

"I remembered him having lipstick on his collar at the training segment and something she said to me a few weeks back about the budget."

Teagan lifted the headpiece out of Spider's hand, checking the range and watching movement from around the corner. Feeling her phone vibrate, she grabbed it off the seat and saw a message from Gregory.

Gregory: Check your email for the link.

Teagan: Thanks.

FIFTEEN

"I got a visual of inside the building. Make sure someone stays on Sandra." Teagan closed her messages and went to her email account. Clicking on the link, she got a clear picture of the front, rear, alleyway, and inside of the bank vault.

"How does it look?" Daughtrey approached with his gun ready.

"I see at least three in the vault and two at the van," Teagan replied, holding the phone up for them to see.

"I'll take it inside," Daughtrey stated, following along with Teagan.

"Great. Spider, handle the two near the van. Take two guys with you."

Everyone nodded in agreement and went their separate ways. Teagan stood against the wall, checking her gun again, motioning for backup to follow as she ducked across, behind some cars, and slipped in next to the bank building. Scanning the live camera footage, Teagan peered at the movements of the robbers, while they bagged up contents of the vault. Biting her bottom lip, Teagan closed her eyes and counted down from five, calculating the time it'd take to get in and out without any of her team getting killed. As the director, she didn't need to go in on missions like these, but when it hit close to home, she took it upon herself to be in the field with her men to show them she was willing to go through war.

"Daughtrey, you're next to me. Tony and Eddie, focus on the rear." Pointing at the security guard to be quiet, Daughtrey picked the lock off the door using his tools. Teagan signaled for the older security guard to head out of the room to safety. Glancing around the room, they saw it was mostly empty with a few employees lying on the floor tied up. The bank was over ten thousand square feet with high ceilings, open space for seating, and cubicles separate from bank tellers. Easing down the hall quietly, Teagan held her gun up as they tread through the hallway and opened each door to see if anyone was left. Daughtrey asked Tony to get the two employees out of the building while the robbers continued packing money up in their bags.

"Let's go! We have two minutes left," a voice called out. Heart pounding, Teagan held her arm out, stopping anyone from parading further in through the commotion. Glancing up, Teagan noticed the mirror at the corner of the vault, seeing two men packing and one on the lookout in the right corner.

"One minute," the guy spoke again.

"Freeze! Put your hands up," Teagan shouted, aiming her gun. Not listening to the instructions, all three guys, wearing all black from ski masks to gloves, blasted off shots toward who they assumed was the police.

Pop! Pop!

Dropping down to the floor behind the island in the

vault, Teagan peered around the room as more bullets whizzed by her head.

"Fuck you!" a gruff voice giving out demands said. Thinking he was the one in charge, she tried to reason with him. Daughtrey hit one of the guys in the arm from close range. The guy screamed in pain and dropped his gun. Standing no more than five-nine, he charged toward Daughtrey when a third shot went through his head.

"You killed him!" Vanya shouted, grabbing a bag of money from the ground, and peered toward the other door in the room.

"Vanya, we need to go." Sergei's heart pounded at his plan falling apart in front of his eyes. Going to jail wasn't in his plans for today, and Maksim promised this was an easy spot.

Pop! Pop!

"Don't move." Teagan squinted her left eye and shot the shorter guy in the foot.

"Ahhggghhh!" Vanya almost fell on the ground, but the leader of the three pushed him in front of himself, blocking Teagan and Daughtrey.

"Not today, sugar." Sergei grinned, shoving his partner in front of them and pushing the emergency exit door that led outside. Tony and the team eased up to the suspect slowly as lay on the ground with blood dripping from every area of his body. Checking his pulse, he shook his head.

"Call for the cleanup crew," Daughtrey commanded, following Teagan.

Opening the door, Daughtrey glanced back and forth, left to right, with his gun. He saw the suspect running toward the van carrying a bag of money.

"Stop!" Teagan yelled, ready to shoot. Not complying,

he ran near the back of the van when Spider shot back at them.

"Vanya and Anthony are dead," Sergei spoke, returning fire toward the back alley and tossing the money in the back of the van.

"We need to get out of here, Sergei. They killed Ivan," his other partner Ulan said and held onto the passenger side door.

"Hold on." Sergei put the van in reverse, busting through barricades of signs and cars. He turned the car into traffic ducking bullets, not making a dent in the bulletproof windshield and side mirrors. Vanya leaned out the window and shot back as Sergei sped up, not caring if anyone got hurt as he drove through the red light. All of a sudden, the traffic light went out, forcing cars to stall and pile up. Teagan jumped in the car next, yelling to follow the van.

"They're getting away." Teagan slammed her hand on the dashboard.

Although they caught who was behind the robbery, it was still going to be a dead end. If the two in the van tried to fire back, this would end up being another front-page problem they didn't need with reporters on the front porch of her house asking questions. Teagan was certain her team was the most elite to end these situations with less bodies than the average police chase. At the same time, it could play in her favor to show what Duncan did go behind the backs of the American people.

Lifting her phone out of her pocket, she redialed Gregory's number. It rang in her ear as she pointed her index finger forward to stay on top of the robbers.

"You're on the news, Teagan," Gregory answered when the phone clicked.

"I need helicopters on the car ahead of us, Gregory."

"You want the police in on this?"

"Yeah, we have two dead and two in chase."

"Tell me the tags."

"More than likely stolen, but 4EFGJS Bronx Security Company."

Daughtrey heard typing on the other end.

"Dammit! They're getting on the highway," Daughtrey shouted.

"Gregory!" Teagan shouted, impatient.

"Arriving in ten minutes. I'm patched into the police scanner. I'll keep you updated," Gregory mentioned, ending the call. Teagan's hand felt sweaty, her throat dry from dodging gunfire and trying to keep a bomb from going off.

"Fuck!" Daughtrey avoided hitting another car as they moved out of the way. Staring out the window, Teagan saw a round of police cars lined up.

"What do you want to do?" Daughtrey questioned.

"Do what you have to."

Daughtrey nodded. "Buckle up."

Teagan reached behind her and grabbed the shotgun. Leaning out the window, she steadied her arm with the gun, squinted, and shot the tire of the black van. A loud pop caused some pieces of the tire to fly off, and the car shifted left to right. She aimed for the left tire, sending it spiraling out of control. In turn, Sergei hit the brakes to slow down. The helicopter continued riding overhead, and Teagan blew out a breath and sent another shot to the driver's side tire. Sergei turned the steering wheel, pissed at how things turned out from this job. He got the car over to the side of the embankment with Daughtrey pulling in a few feet away.

"I got Sergei," Teagan gave direction to Daughtrey.

"Eyes wide open." He eased out on the driver's side with his gun ready, monitoring every movement.

"Get out of the car with your hands up!" she called. One side of the passenger door opened.

"You guys got eyes on them?" Teagan asked Daughtrey.

"Eyes and ears."

Backup came next to her, holding the passenger door for her to come around and stride up to the vehicle.

"Keep your hands up and step out of the vehicle," she demanded. Vanya looked at Sergei, nodded, and he swiftly jumped out of the driver's side. They both fired back at Teagan and the team, until she screamed and shot him in the chest.

Daughtrey fired more shots into Sergei's body until his clip was empty.

"You good!" Daughtrey shouted, coming up to the side of the vehicle and kicking the gun away. He leaned down and checked his pulse as blood dripped on the ground.

"Clear." Teagan slid the back door of the van open. Seeing the bags of money, she lifted them and passed them over to the police.

"Get forensics to look into this."

Teagan strolled around toward Daughtrey and took Sergei's ID out of his hands.

"Related to Maksim."

"I won't be surprised if all of them are related."

She waved up toward the helicopter to leave.

"You making the call?"

Running how the conversation may go in her head, she quickly pulled her phone out to give the confirmation they'd been waiting on.

"Hello," Christian answered.

"Hey." Teagan watched as the coroner came over to take photos of the bodies.

"Is it done?" Christian spoke on the other end of the line.

"Yes, I'm coming home."

"I guess the kids need to know that their mom won't be retiring anytime soon."

"I'm sorry."

"I know you better than you know yourself, Teagan."

"How so?" Teagan clenched her teeth.

"You want to save the world, even if you know you can't."

For years, Teagan told Christian the reason she served her country was to save the world. Even knowing it could leave her family without her would never cause her to slow down until she had CJ. Seeing all three kids in the line of drama only made her go harder.

"Where are you?" Teagan muttered, getting inside the car and closing the door.

"Driving home with the kids. We have private escorts going through traffic."

"Are the kids scared?"

"Surprisingly, they think we're like royalty right now." Teagan chuckled.

"I'll be home soon."

"Be safe."

"You too."

The door to the driver's side opened, and Daughtrey got inside and turned the radio on low as they sat waiting to head back home.

"Is everything good?"

"Yeah, local PD is handling things so we can head out."

"Good, I plan on taking a vacation for real this time."

Daughtrey turned the left signal light on and eased into traffic from behind the bank van back.

"Are you going out of the country?"

"I think so. Christian and the kids have been through enough. Time for me to go back into mom mode."

"Let me guess, France."

"What makes you think of France?"

"You look like the type of woman that loves all that French food and museums." Daughtrey winked, speeding to the off ramp.

"I do love museums and French food, but I'm thinking of London as a vacation spot."

Slowing down at the light, Daughtrey cracked his knuckles and yawned as Teagan sat back with her eyes closed in the seat.

"I admire you, Teagan."

One eye popped open.

"Huh?"

"I don't think I would've come back in the way you did. I know Broderick's an asshole, but he's always been for the team."

"Are you trying to convince me to not kick him off the team by buttering me up?"

"As long as I've known you, no one could bribe you to do anything."

"Then what are you saying?"

"Take the vacation and think about if you want to be in this forever."

"I can say the same thing to you."

"This is my life."

"Bigger things in life are more important than The Firm."

Daughtrey continued driving back to the city, tapping his fingers on the steering wheel.

"Probably but will never know," Daughtrey replied.

"The Firm lets you believe you're in control of your life. You'll learn one day."

I HOPE you enjoyed Teagan's story so far. Please also check out "**Agent Red (Fatal Enemy) Teagan Stone Book 5" here** https://books2read.com/u/bxeo1q with a host of characters intertwined.

Check out free short here ***"The Firm"*** https://payhip.com/b/py7S

Grab Boxset "**Agent Red 1-3**" here https://payhip.com/b/1KcxY

AGENT RED (FATAL ENEMY) TEAGAN
STONE BOOK 5

Enemies come in all forms, and Teagan Stone is ready for battle, not thinking of the consequences for going to war with her ultimate rival. Can she turn back the clock or will this lead her to finally leave The Firm before it destroys her from within?

MIRROR OF LIES BOOK 1

Alison and Jessica were the best of friends of middle and high school. Fifteen years later, Jessica, now an up-and-coming journalist, learns that Alison has been killed in a car accident. But that's not the most troubling part of this tragedy.

Alison died with a secret that only she, Jessica, and a small group of friends know. Her fear is that secret didn't die with her friend.

If it didn't, what does that mean for her and the others who know what happened all those years ago?

READING ORDER OF SERIES

Agent Red-Fatal Memory Book 1
    https://books2read.com/u/4j2PYX
    Agent Red-Fatal Target Book 2
    https://books2read.com/u/bWP8Jq
    Agent Red-Fatal Crime Book 3
    https://books2read.com/u/mZadZJ
    Agent Red-Fatal Justice Book 4
    https://books2read.com/u/mqo7wd
    Agent Red-Fatal Enemy Book 5
    https://books2read.com/u/bxeo1q

ACKNOWLEDGMENTS

I want to thank my team, who helps me behind the scenes, from my editors to my test readers and graphic designers, and the list goes on. I truly appreciate each of you for keeping me on my toes.

ABOUT THE AUTHOR

Ava S. King writes mystery, psychological crime thrillers, international espionage thrillers, political and action/adventure novels. Her debut novel, Agent Red Fatal Memory became a huge hit with 1oo BestSellers, Top Indie Favorite. 1oo Debut release on all digital platforms. Born and raised in TN, filmmaker and lover of all things mystery and suspense. In addition to writing, Ava loves bringing her novels to life on the bigscreen starting with Agent Red series.

If you want to know when the next book will come out, please visit my website at http://www.authoravasking.com, where you can sign up to receive an email for her next release.

Agent Red Fatal Memory Book 1 Teagan Stone
Agent Red Fatal Target Book 2 Teagan Stone
Agent Red Fatal Crime Book 3 Teagan Stone
Agent Red Fatal Justice Book 4 Teagan Stone
Thank you so much for reading and if you enjoyed the crazy ride and decide to leave a review I'd truly appreciate the support.

WHAT'S NEXT?

Want to know what happens next? Follow me at the links below to catch the next release.

Thank you so much for reading, and if you enjoyed the crazy ride and decided to leave a review, we'd truly appreciate the support. Reviews are the lifeblood of the publishing world. They're read, appreciated, and needed. Please consider taking the time to leave a few words on Goodreads or BookBub.

Sign up for updates and sneak peeks at the sites below:
www.authoravasking.com